PRAISE FOR OUR KINGDOM OF DUST

"Our Kingdom Of Dust is a fantastic and wonderfully written debut novel from Leonard Kinsey. A powerful narrative with some of the weirdest characters you'll ever meet, it's like a Palahniuk novel high on Pixie Dust, with a dash of the dark side of Disney thrown in for good measure. Suspenseful and hilarious, this is a must read for everyone who's always suspected there's a seedy underbelly to all things Disney."
—Jeff Heimbuch, *Miceage.com*

"A fantastic story about a man who looks to his childhood for salvation from a life that has turned on him, only to find that things aren't always as expected (or remembered). *Our Kingdom of Dust* is an emotion-provoking read, written in classic Kinsey style."
—Brett Bennett, *WDWFanboys.com*

"Kinsey breaks new ground with a tale about addiction – mental, emotional and physical – in his look at one Disney fan's journey back to the memories of his youth. Anyone who has revisited their childhood stomping grounds and found disturbing changes will relate, as will anyone who has fallen in love so quickly that they couldn't explain it. *Our Kingdom of Dust* is a true page-turner that will keep you on the edge of your seat until the final word."
—George Taylor, *Imaginerding.com*

"Leonard Kinsey is at it again, this time exposing the dark side of Guests and Cast Members who'll do anything for a taste of 'Happily Ever After'. *Our Kingdom of Dust* is one scary ride!"
—Ron Schneider, author of *From Dreamer to Dreamfinder*

OUR KINGDOM OF DUST
LEONARD KINSEY

BAMBOO FOREST
PUBLISHING

Copyright 2012, Leonard Kinsey

Cover Design: Pentakis Dodecahedron
Cover Photo: Alan Partlow
Cover Model: Draven Star
Book Design: Jonas Kyle-Sidell
Editor/Fact Checker: Hugh Allison

ISBN: 978-0-9854706-0-9

Published by Bamboo Forest Publishing
First Printing: May, 2012

Visit us Online at:
www.bambooforestpublishing.com

is what's been lurking under the calm, quiet exterior. This is the reason for the scared itch in the back of my brain whenever I've been around him lately. This is what his tattoos were covering up.

He looks at the splinters from the base of the statue, jutting out of flesh that looks like it was hit with a shotgun blast, takes a swig from the bottle of wine he's holding, and goes, "Dude, Disney and shit! I mean, Walt-fucking-Disney, right?"

"Sure, Disney," I say.

I can't stop staring at the Mouse Ears on her head. The b[...] is seeping through them, and the felt is glistening more [...] plastic ears. I'm flashing back to white fur, intestine[...]

This is worse. I just kissed her this afternoo[...] love with her all over again this afternoon[...] is bashed open and her arm looks lik[...] grinder.

I turn, vomit again, and [...] gonna do?"

Jay looks at me [...] all the characters o[...] And he says, "Hey, [...] you're really leaving the[...] Call the goddamned polic[...]

We stare at each other a[...] that this guy is just flat out [...] either, like I'd deluded myself i[...] batshit insane.

"You're an asshole," I say, wiping t[...]

I'm not surprised at what now [...] inevitability of it all, but this wasn't how [...] turn out. This isn't what I came here for.

PROLOGUE

—It's a clear, beautiful night, and I'm sauntering down The BoardWalk, high on life. Lights from nearby buildings are twinkling and reflecting off the lake. Small crowds surround the street entertainers, and I hear kids laughing at some gag I've probably seen twenty times but would still laugh at if I saw again. The scent of funnel cakes mixes with the exhaust of the boats, forming an aromatic concoction unique to this place. It's a nice smell. A surrey bike's bell clangs as it careens past me, nearly knocking over an old lady on its uncontrolled ride down the bridge. I smile, and turn off onto a wooded path, where Spanish moss glows in the moonlight and toads croak. There are gators, too, probably lots of them. And snakes. Poisonous snakes. But I don't see them, so I don't think about them. Right now my thoughts are blanketed by the face of a girl, and a kiss, and everything that might come of that kiss.

Before I know it I'm standing in front of my suite at The Beach Club. I'm going to have to tell Jay I'm leaving. To say he will be less than pleased is an understatement. But I don't see them, so I don't think [...] I'm jolted out of my fantasyland when it dawns on me that Maybe it can wait until tomorrow, though.

I push my card into the slot on the lock. It beeps. I open the door and step inside.

There are bloody footprints on the floor, from the v[...] the bedroom. My bedroom. There are bloody handprin[...] bedroom door.

"Jay, are you okay?" I call out to the guy who has been crashing on my couch for the past few weeks. "Did you cut yourself on something?"

The bedroom door is cracked. I push it open.

I look down and see Lisa's contorted body. There's a bunch of blood, and it's all smeared on the wall and dripping down onto the carpet.

I try to blink it away, but there it is. Blood everywhere.

As near as I can figure, Jay smashed her head against the cheap drywall a few times until he put a hole through it. Then I guess he decided to stab her in the shoulder with his stolen brass Cinderella Castle statue, parts of which are laying in bloodied pieces on the floor. The rest, a combination of jagged metal and splintered wood, is still stuck in Lisa's shoulder. What I can't figure out is why he felt the need to put my Haunted Mansion Mouse Ears on her blood-caked head.

A ripped bag of sparkling white powder is strewn across the floor next to the bed. Jay had sworn he didn't have any more of the stuff. Obviously he'd lied. The powder is all over the place an—

There's also at least $10K in hundreds scattered—

mixing with the blood. It looks like blood paste.

Jay is sitting on the bed, half naked, an—

room. A lot of those are soaked through with blo—

it's a tribute to the fucking genius of—

like that. He's cursing, which he ne—

convinced this simply isn't real—

to be at work. This sort of—

But then I think of—

Jay turns to—

all of his s—

Techn—

"H

1

—Born Blaine McKinnon, July 1976. I took after my mom in the looks department. My friends always said she was really hot, and were always coming over hoping to catch a glimpse of her sunbathing out in the backyard. Perverts. Like her, I'm short and skinny, with freckles and brown eyes, but with my dad's crazy curly brown hair. Above-average but not someone you're going to notice walking down a crowded street. So, yeah, none of my issues came from any self-esteem problems, at least not regarding my looks.

From my dad, I received what is probably my only major vice: I curse like a sailor. He was so good at it, he'd make f-bombs sound like poetry. And he was never embarrassed about letting a string of profanities fly from his mouth, no matter where he was, or who he was around. I loved that about him.

Mom was a hair stylist and Dad was a house painter. Real salt of the earth people, my parents were. They moved down to Florida in the early 70s to get away from the drugs and crime in Baltimore. Considering how there wasn't anything in Pinellas County aside from orange groves, I guess they figured it was a safer place to raise a kid. For the most part, they were right.

They did okay for themselves, too. With the Florida housing boom my dad had all the work he could handle, and the 80s were a fucking godsend for anyone in the hair styling business. I always had the best hair in school – my mom could feather with the best of them.

I remember the first time they took me to Walt Disney World. I was four, and it was the summer before I was supposed to start kindergarten. I already knew how to read and write, so they were thinking of skipping me ahead to first grade, but my mom wanted me around kids my own age. I'm glad she did, because I've always been short, and was harassed a bit about it over the years. If I'd gone through school with kids a year older than me the teasing would've been a lot worse, and maybe I would've ended up with an inferiority complex or something.

Anyway, my grandparents were visiting from Illinois, and we all went to Disney together, driving the two hours from Palm Harbor to Orlando cramped into my dad's Dodge Omni. The AC was busted, and I remember everyone being cranky and sniping at each other. But I also remember that the second they stepped through that tunnel under the railroad station and saw Main Street, they all had huge grins on their faces. It wasn't called The Magic Kingdom for nothing. The impression that this place could make people happy, despite all odds, stuck with me.

My parents must have had the same feeling, too, because from then on the three of us went back to Walt Disney World every year, and then twice a year, and then we got "Three Season Salute" passes which let us go as much as we wanted during the "slow" months. I felt like I had the happiest times of my life there, so it was no wonder I longed to return when I discovered adulthood wasn't all it was cracked up to be.

I truly believe it was EPCOT Center that put me on the path to becoming a millionaire, at least in a roundabout way. The park opened in 1982 and had a bunch of rides and exhibits showcasing Walt Disney's utopian vision of the future. EPCOT was an acronym for "Experimental Prototype Community of Tomorrow". It was kinda like a permanent world's fair, and six-year-old me figured it was easily the coolest place in the universe. My favorite ride, Horizons, opened in 1983. It slowly moved you through a vision of the future where technology made everyone's lives awesome. There was a part at the end where you got to push a picture on your ride vehicle to "choose your own future". You could pick from space, desert, or undersea living, and then you'd fly through these futuristic scenes, sorta like a low-rent motion simulator. My parents and I used to go on the ride at least three times every trip so we could choose each of the future scenes. It was "our" ride, for sure.

Point is, I made my fortune working with computers, and it was EPCOT Center that got me hooked on the things. Obsessed, actually. The first time I went there and saw how these huge servers were controlling everything in the whole park... damn. I begged for a computer for months after that, and finally got a Radio Shack TRS-80 for my eighth birthday. I lovingly referred to it as a "Rat Shack Trash 80" due to its propensity to break all the time. But I learned how to fix the break-downs. I taught myself how to solder capacitors, to replace worn out fans, and to upgrade memory. It all just made sense. It clicked. And once I really started getting into that computer, pulling out its guts, figuring out what everything did, tinkering with various parts to improve performance... well, nothing else seemed to matter. Or, more accurately, other things did matter, but computers were always there for me, calm, sane, logical, non-judgmental, and always willing to do exactly what I told them to do.

In the early 90s, when I was in high school, it seemed like all of a sudden everyone owned a computer. A lot of those early PCs weren't ventilated very well so stuff would always overheat or burn up. And the pre-Windows 98 operating systems didn't warn you about deleting critical files so people were always losing important shit while trying to free up space on their miniscule hard drives. Since I was the only person anyone knew who understood how PCs worked, I started getting calls all the time from friends and relatives, asking if I could do them a HUGE favor (they always said HUGE) and come fix their broken computer. My dad told me to "stop letting those fucking leeches take advantage of you," so pretty quickly I started charging for my services, and before

I knew it, I was in the computer repair business. In the summer after my junior year I took over the basement of my parents' condo, incorporated, and hired an employee.

CompuTech was born, and I made over $10,000 that summer.

It felt good to have my own money and be able to buy whatever I wanted. And there was something addictive about using my brain to figure out what was wrong with a computer, fixing it, and then being a fucking "Office Park Super Hero". The receptionists at these places particularly seemed to dig this schtick, and I lost my virginity to one such hottie on the CEO's desk after a late night of server patching.

I certainly had no desire to go back to school at the end of the summer, but begrudgingly did so, while still trying to meet the needs of the client base I'd built up. Between my AP classes at school and the demands of the business, I was maybe getting four hours of sleep every night. Parties? Dances? Dates? No time. Friends? Movies? Music? Nope. Disney? Are you kidding? No way I could be gone for a whole day. I turned into a hermit, completely unaware of everything kids my age were into. I'd try to go out with girls, but couldn't relate to anything they were saying. I didn't know the bands or TV shows they'd blather on about, and they had no concept of what it meant to run a business. Apparently I waited too long to ask Susan Gibbons (the one girl in my AP Calc class who actually kinda got what I was doing) to the prom. My so-called best friend at the time, Ricky Lu, asked her instead, and ended up fucking her in his parents' van after the dance.

Ricky Lu was the sort of friend who always does everything you do, except wants to one-up you at it. When I tried out for the football team in middle school, he tried out, too, and tackled me repeatedly during the scrimmage. When I took up guitar and started a band Sophomore year of high school, he learned bass, begged to join the band, and then "accidentally" destroyed my amp right before our first gig. And when I liked a girl, oh, let's say Susan Gibbons, he talked shit about me behind my back and then fucked her.

The one thing he couldn't do, though, was be a successful businessman. He just didn't have it in him. He wasn't smart enough, he wasn't driven enough, and he was too much of an asshole to maintain loyal clients. And the fact that he couldn't beat me at something killed him. Killed him for years, apparently.

I don't know why we stayed friends. I was easy to take advantage of, and far too forgiving. He'd always make me feel guilty for getting mad when he fucked shit up for me. He'd go on about how he hadn't done it on purpose and then act all hurt that I'd accuse him of such a thing. What a slimeball he was. What a loser I was. We were a perfect match.

Anyway, after my senior year I had a choice: continue the business or go to college. I'd been accepted to Stanford, Duke, and Vanderbilt. My parents wanted me to go to college, to try to regain some sort of normal adolescence. They were right, of course, but I just didn't know if I could turn down the money I was making.

Unfortunately, I never had the chance to fight it out with them. Early that summer they both died in a car accident. Someone in one of those goddamned Home Depot moving trucks, the ones that they let you rent by the hour but don't give you any training on, literally drove over top of my parents' car. I guess the load the truck was carrying was too heavy, and the brakes didn't stop as quickly as the driver expected. Since the truck was so high off the ground it didn't simply run into the back of my parents' car. Instead, it went right over it, shearing off the top and killing my mom immediately. My dad lingered for a bit longer. Long enough for the paramedics to get there, anyway. The main paramedic on the scene said my dad's last words were, no joke, "This shit wouldn't have happened if they'd fucking built monorails everywhere." Helluva guy.

Did their deaths mess me up? Yeah, but not necessarily right then and there. I shed a few tears wishing I'd gone to EPCOT Center with them more often – they'd always invite me to go but I'd always turn them down. And a few days after the funeral I was packing up their stuff and found their still unexpired yearly passes in my dad's wallet. Knowing that the passes would never be used again choked me up a bit. But when you're that young somehow things are easier to deal with, or at least, easier to push aside, to deal with later. So that's pretty much what I did. Pushed it aside, covered it up with work, left the emotions to ferment and rot until sometime later, sometime when I'd maybe have the time and inclination to deal with them properly. That... was a mistake.

All I know was that after the funeral, after everything had been taken care of, I had one blindingly intense focus for my life: making CompuTech an enormous success. I took the insurance money and used part of it to get a government security clearance, because I knew there were some extremely lucrative contracts out there, and I wanted to be a part of it. What a fucking involved, tedious, annoying process that was. A total invasion of privacy. I felt like they were anally raping my life.

But, the security clearance paid off when CompuTech won a contract to install and network thousands of computers for a major upgrade to the Goddard Space Flight Center in Greenbelt, Maryland, not far from where my parents used to live. It was a crapshoot bid, and I never honestly expected to get it. But once again, EPCOT Center intervened: turns out the head of the project, a guy named Sam Mason, was also an EPCOT Center junkie, and the SMRT-1 robot in CommuniCore had kickstarted his interest in robotics, leading to an eventual career at Goddard. We bonded immediately during my initial presentation, and I guess I bid low enough to make me a shoe-in. Sam took me under his wing and we actually became pretty good friends.

I remember he called me over to his house one time to fix his webcam, and he opened the door wearing nothing but a loosely drawn robe. Inside was a "friend" of his, a big hairy bear of a guy, sitting at the computer, dressed only in tighty-whities. After a few seconds I figured out that they needed me to fix their webcam so they could broadcast their buttsex across the Internet. Awkward! Sam seemed a bit embarrassed, but I just laughed it off, fixed their webcam, and told him he owed me one. The next day a hot brunette Strip-O-Gram arrived at my house. Sam must have given her a big tip in advance, because I got a handjob out of that one!

A few years later Sam died of AIDS.

So, anyway, once I found out I won the Goddard bid I packed up everything I owned, moved to Maryland, and lived and breathed computers. A few months later Ricky Lu moved up from Florida and became my office manager. We leased a small place in Baltimore and used the cachet of the government job to bring in a ton of clients, selling small to medium sized businesses on the idea that they didn't need a full-time IT guy when my team could come in one day a week and take care of any computer problems they were having. Within a year I had thirty techs driving all over the Baltimore/DC area, fixing computers and making me a buttload of money.

Business boomed, but the twenty-hour days never stopped, and I had no social life. That first year in Maryland I had a brief liaison with my receptionist, Connie. That "relationship" lasted a week, after which she promptly quit and sued me for sexual harassment. She didn't win, but it was humiliating having my genitalia described in graphic detail to a jury.

A few months after the Connie incident, Ricky Lu decided to start his own company and sabotaged CompuTech by planting a virus on my network, taking me down for a week. He used this as an opportunity to steal dozens of my clients, and half of my employees. Typical. His company folded eighteen month later, and when he came crawling back for a job I told him to go fuck himself.

These betrayals only reinforced my decision to devote all of my energy to the business.

I did get a dog. A huge Siberian Husky. I found him huddled in a kennel at a shelter, a few days away from being put to sleep. His hair was gray and knotted, and it seemed like being cramped in that cage had sucked out his will to live. According to the shelter he had a major problem with children, since he'd been mercilessly abused by neighborhood kids over the summer while left chained to a fence all day by his owners. No families wanted to adopt him because he'd lunge whenever anyone under four feet tall walked by his cage, but I hated the little parasites, too, so it was a match made in heaven. I fucking loved that dog. I used to put a red handkerchief around his neck. He knew he looked awesome with that handkerchief on. I named him Sam, in honor of the only other true friend I'd had in Maryland. Fucking badass dog, that Sam.

And then, before I knew it, I was thirty. I owned two office buildings, employed nearly a hundred people, and was worth at least three million. I was a success, and success doesn't go unnoticed in the business world. AlphaZero, a multinational tech company hoping to expand into the Baltimore area, swooped down and offered me a five million dollar buyout package. The client base I'd worked so hard to build for the past thirteen years, the brilliant employees I'd scouted and trained… they wanted all of it. Surprisingly, they didn't want the real estate, which at this point was easily worth another million. They had their own office in Silver Spring, and would be relocating everyone there.

Well, my employees weren't thrilled about any of that. First off, they didn't want to make the lengthy commute from Baltimore to Silver Spring. I had to admit to them that yes, it was a shitty drive, and that yes, if they wanted to keep their jobs at the company it was a burden they'd have to bear.

Grumbles. Unrest. Anger.

The employees who'd been there a while figured they were owed something for helping to make the company successful enough to get it bought out in the first place. And they weren't wrong. They probably did deserve a cut for their years of hard work, over and above their pretty hefty paychecks. But still, they hadn't been the ones working twenty hour days for thirteen years. And they hadn't been the ones taking all the financial risks. Taking out loans that maybe couldn't ever be paid back. Buying the newest tech equipment, not knowing if it'd pay off. Or hiring the best and brightest in the area, never sure if the customers would give a shit. So, yeah, the guys who'd been around for a while had helped make the company a success, but they weren't living and breathing it 24/7. They hadn't given up their youth for it.

Regardless, I decided to throw a big going away party at my house. Kick ass catering (fucking kangaroo nuggets!), open bar, complimentary limos, and a live band. It was an amazing party, and for a few hours it seemed like everything was okay. People were happy. They were having a great time. I'd even invited Ricky Lu in an attempt at reconciliation, trying to be the bigger guy. We talked a bit, and it seemed like he was also having a great time eating all my food and walking around swigging from a bottle of Grey Goose. For a few hours I hoped that maybe we could be friends again.

Then it came time to give out the bonuses....

I thought I was being ultra-generous. Nobody, not even the guy who'd only been there a week, got less than $2K. A few people got as much as $25K. I gave Ricky Lu $5K! Altogether I gave out a little over $500K. I expected people to be thrilled, and I even made a little speech. But as the alcohol flowed and the night wore on, they turned on me. The fucking ungrateful bastards turned on me. I kinda had a feeling things weren't right as they filtered out of the party at the end of the night. Some of them had shit-eating grins on their faces. Some just looked angry. The rest wouldn't look me in the eye at all. Ricky Lu was nowhere to be found. I never saw him leave.

It was when the last guest left that I began to realize the extent of the damage. Somebody shit on my bed. Someone else stole a pocket watch that had belonged to my great-great-grandfather. My gas tank was filled with sugar, and my tires were slashed. A few of my employees, obviously planning this for a while, dumped bags of concrete into my pool. Childish, annoying, stupid pranks. Those, I could understand. Those I could forgive. But what they, or should I say he, did to Sam....

Fuck, my heart breaks just thinking about it.

I can't prove for a fact it was Ricky Lu, and the police didn't seem interested in figuring it out. But it was fucking Ricky Lu.

I'd put Sam out in his fenced off area in the backyard early in the evening, before anyone showed up. He had a kick ass doghouse that was the size of a shed, and even had air conditioning and heat. Outside of the doghouse was a genuine fire hydrant I'd bought off eBay, and a big maple tree where squirrels would hang out, taunting him from the upper branches. It was a nice area for him. It was his domain, his own little section of the world, and he loved it. He was so happy out there....

And I'm fucking crying again.

Anyway, after everyone had left, and after spending ten minutes trying to figure out exactly what the fuck had happened to my pool, I finally made it to Sam's house, coming along the path to the back of it. I called him, but he didn't come out. I opened the back door, but he wasn't in there. Had someone let him out? I was seething. But I knew even if they had let him out he wouldn't have gone far. I called for him again.

Nothing.

I walked around to the front of the doghouse, and that's when I saw him hanging from the maple tree.

He was tied to the lowest thick branch, legs dangling in the wind. Tied to the branch with his bandana, which was bright, bright red in that moonlight. There was more red on his fluffy white fur, and as my eyes drifted down I saw his intestines hanging out, hanging down almost to the ground, the blood glistening in that blue light. All I could do was wonder if he been hanged or gutted first. I didn't know which was worse.

I walked over to him and touched his flank.

He twitched.

I jumped back a mile, and then in slow motion ran over to him again.

The fucker was still alive.

I don't remember exactly how, but somehow I got him down, and he was on the ground, not really doing anything, not whimpering or trying to move or anything. Just looking at me.

For a second I considered taking him to the Pet E.R., but I

couldn't stand it, couldn't stand having him alive like that, even for another minute.

Was that selfish of me? Could they have saved him? I don't think so, but the thought still haunts me....

I ran into my garage, searched frantically for an axe, couldn't find one, grabbed a shovel, and ran back to Sam.

"Sam, buddy, I'm so fucking...." I broke off, not able to continue, seeing his eyes looking up at me.

I bent down and kissed his head, then stood up and brought the blade of the shovel down on his neck. I missed and hit his back, cutting his spinal cord. He let out a quiet yelp.

As quickly as I could I struck him again with the blade of the shovel, right at the base of his skull, and severed his head.

I killed my only friend.

And that's when I had my breakdown.

I have no recollection of the week that followed. All I knew, coming out of it, was that I was rich and filled with rage and hate, because after all of those years of hard work I had nothing, except for some stupid number in my bank account. My life had been spent building something that was sold with a stroke of a key. I'd been working nonstop since I was sixteen, and now had nothing to work towards, no purpose. I was adrift, my youth was lost, my life was empty, and I was alone. I was utterly, completely alone. No friends, no wife, no kids, not even a dog. It had all been sacrificed for cash. What a stupid fucking life I'd lived.

When I looked back over the years, it seemed as if the only times I was ever truly happy were when I was with someone, be it hanging with Sam (the guy) or Sam (the dog), or going to Walt Disney World with my parents. But they were all gone...

Except for Walt Disney World. It was still there. The only thing in my life that had made me happy and still existed was Walt Disney World. Main Street. EPCOT Center. Monorails. Horizons. I hadn't been there since 1993. Hadn't even really thought about it for years. Fuck.

So I did what any depressed, non-rational human would do and booked a ticket to Walt Disney World. Reserved a one-bedroom concierge suite at The Beach Club, indefinitely. I was surprised they let me do that, actually. But I didn't know how long I'd be there. All I knew was I had to be there, and that something... no, everything, had to change.

2

—The limo dropped me off at BWI. I checked my five bags and knocked back four Heinekens at the bar by the gate before boarding the plane, first class. Already drunk, I proceeded to order three more gin and tonics during the ninety minute flight to Orlando International. I stumbled off the plane and somehow made it onto the second-rate monorail to baggage claim, where a guy was supposed to be waiting to pick me up. I looked around, saw a bunch of dudes in suits and stupid hats, but was completely incapable of focusing on the writing on any of the signs. I panicked.

"My name is Blaine McKinnon!" I yelled at the top of my voice.

People turned to stare. Nobody said anything.

"I'm drunk and in need of a limo!"

A lady covered her kid's ears. That pissed me off for some reason, so I yelled at her, louder still, "What's your problem lady? I just need my fucking limo!"

Her kid, a cute little girl dressed as Snow White, smiled innocently. I twirled around like a fucking ballerina, pulled out my wallet, and handed the kid $100.

"Shazam!" I said to the kid. "Put it in savings for the therapy you'll need after having this bitch as a mother."

The mother gasped, the kid giggled, and I twirled again, tried to jump and click my heels together, and fell flat on my face. I heard some claps and laughter, so I stood up, bowed, and was suddenly whisked off my feet by a large pair of hands. I was being held sideways by a thick arm. The black coat sleeve was pushed up and I saw Princess Jasmine staring at me. I puked on black, shiny, patent leather shoes and promptly passed out.

3

—An article I found on Google a few days later:

Tattooed Disney Fan Reveals Incredible Memorabilia Collection

The Orlando Sentinel
February 21, 2007

Easily one of the most widely recognized and infamous Disney fans, Jason "Jay" Montgomery, better known among Cast Members and Guests as "The Disney Tattoo Guy", has made headlines around the world for his stunning Disney tattoos. They cover nearly every inch of his body aside from his hands and face - altogether he has over 1600 separate tattoos, ranging from Disney characters such as Mickey and Goofy, to pictures of ride vehicles, to a Cast Member nametag on his upper left chest.

But Jay's love of Disney doesn't just extend to tattoos. He has a massive museum-quality collection of Disney memorabilia that he's spent years acquiring. It numbers over 20,000 pieces and according to Jay is worth millions.

"The Disney Family is gathering artifacts for a museum they're going to open," smiles Jay as he tells one of his favorite stories. "They'd heard I had in my collection a rare 16mm wartime Disney Studios short that they simply couldn't find in their archives. I was happy to lend it to them for duplication..." He grins again. "For a price, of course!"

Jay gives off the impression of being a big kid. He never uses profanity, and speaks with a childish lilt. But he's a big burly man with a trim moustache and a horseshoe-shaped hairline, and he strikes quite a form in his immaculately pressed navy blue suit. However, it's when the clothes come off that his passion and devotion to Disney becomes apparent.

"I don't have any on my face or hands because I'm a limo driver and they want their drivers to look professional," says Jay. "But everywhere else is fair game! I even have them on my private parts," he admits. "Took a while to find someone who would do that for me!"

When asked what Disney artwork he has on his "private parts", Jay becomes coy. "That's only for my special ladyfriends to find out," he says. His grin turns downwards. "So far there have been two wives. They couldn't handle my Disney obsession. Everything is Disney with me, all the time. I only read Disney books, only watch Disney movies, only listen to Disney music. They knew that coming in, but I guess it got to be too much. Their loss! But this new girl I'm dating, she's a Cast Member, so obviously she gets it. I think she might be the one!"

Jay has three kids from his prior marriages. "They were all into my Disney obsession until they got older, and then I guess it started embarrassing them. I had high hopes for my youngest, who is sixteen now. But she ran away a few weeks ago to live with her mother. It's a shame, since now she won't be inheriting all of this," he says, sweeping his arms across the collection that engulfs his house.

"I was twenty-two. It was the day after my dad died," he says when asked when he got his first Disney tattoo. He points to his upper left arm. "Snow White. As a kid I was in love with her. I hit puberty, and it almost became an obsession. Yep, I was obsessed with Snow White, and you know what? I still am!"

"You want to know why I like Disney so much?" he says before the question is asked. "We were kind of poor when I was a kid, so I had to work a lot and missed out on a lot of regular kid stuff. I had a paper route, and worked in my dad's shop, and was home-schooled. My parents were very religious, and very strict, but they did let me watch Disney stuff because they saw Uncle Walt as a wholesome guy. One of the few books I was allowed to read was a Walt Disney biography and I really related to him because his childhood was the same as mine."

"I'm not an educated guy," admits Jay. "But I do okay for myself. When my dad died I sold his business and moved here to Florida so I could be near the parks. My mom, too. She's out in a Tarpon Springs nursing home." He grimaces and then smiles again. "I blew a lot of that money on my collection and tattoos, but my limo driver job is pretty nice, so I get by okay. And I get into the parks for free because all the Cast Members know me, so I'm usually there every day before or after work or on my days off, just walking around. Kids get a kick out of my tattoos, so I always wear sleeveless shirts and shorts. And even though they've never officially said anything, I think The Company likes me being there. Like I'm another one of their entertainers or something."

"Okay," Jay says, getting up and putting on his suit jacket. "Time for the day job!" His outfit completely covers all his tattoos, and he looks, dare say, normal. "Let me know next time you're in the parks. I'll get you in for free, introduce you to everybody, and get you backstage. I'm like a celebrity there!"

4

—I woke up to the *Mary Poppins* soundtrack, Dick Van Dyke's annoying faux-cockney accent pounding my head with each broken syllable, followed by Julie Andrews' nasally whine piercing my brain. I love that soundtrack, but at that moment I don't think I'd ever heard anything more annoying. I wanted to kill the Sherman Brothers.

Even with my eyes shut, I knew I'd puked all over myself. I could smell it. One eye popped open, and sure enough there was a stream of vomit all over my vintage EPCOT Center t-shirt. My only thought was whether the stain was going to come out. I was pissed. My other crusty eye ripped itself open, and I vowed never to drink again.

And then I realized I had no idea where the fuck I was. This was not The Beach Club. But there was Disney shit everywhere. Like, seriously, there was Disney shit all over the fucking place. The pillows I was laying on were shaped like Mickey's head. The blanket on me had a *Lion King* print. The coffee table next to me was a replica of the magic mirror from *Snow White*... which, admittedly, was pretty cool. There were little figurines everywhere. Stuffed animals. Framed art. Tapestries. All Disney.

"Where the fuck am I?" I asked aloud.

"Watch the language, please," answered a soft voice from behind me. I twisted my head and saw a fat guy with a moustache, frowning at me. "You're in my house," he said.

"Who the fuck are you?" I asked, a little louder. I panicked. I was in a fat guy's house. He didn't like cursing. And he had a moustache. This couldn't be good.

"Language, please!" the fat man said, exasperated. "I'm the guy whose shoes you vomited on yesterday."

I focused and saw that he was wearing boxers and a wife-beater, and was covered in tattoos. Creepy.

"I'm the guy whose limo you urinated in. You also vomited there. You vomited a lot, actually. What did you eat yesterday?!"

The tattoos were all Disney. Just like the shit in the house. Weird. But then instead of panicking, I just felt bad, because, yes, I likely had pissed and puked all over this guy's limo.

"Damn, dude," I said, trying to get up and immediately regretting it. The pain in my head was unfathomable. "I'm really, really, honestly sorry about that, and I will fully compensate you for any, uh, damages I might have caused."

I turned my body to get a better look at the fat man and right at that instant he opened the curtains. The light shot from the window, barreled through my bloodshot eye, and exited through the back of my head. The pain was so intense that I was pretty sure the light somehow blew off a chunk of my skull. I fell back onto the sofa.

"Well, I hope so," he started, "because I had to cancel all of my appointments today to get the upholstery professionally cleaned, and...."

I cut him off.

"I would really love to continue this conversation," I said, "and discuss what I owe you, and more importantly, try to figure out what exactly I'm doing in your house. I'm sure it's all very innocent, and that you're a nice man who has no intention of murdering or raping me. But, and I hope I'm not imposing too much here, in order to have that conversation I'm going to need like six ibuprofen and at least two cups of coffee."

My stomach was burning. "And something to eat," I added.

I looked down at my shirt. "This is a rare shirt. Is the stain going to come out?"

My head was pounding to a beat. Specifically, to the beat of *Supercalifragilisticexpialidocious.* "I'm also going to need you to please turn off that music. Thank you. In advance. Seriously, thank you, I'll pay you for everything. I'll pay you to turn off the music. Seriously."

"Give me the shirt," the fat man said.

I pulled off the shirt, threw it in his general direction, plopped back onto the sofa and did the only thing that seemed socially acceptable at that point in time. I turned and fell asleep....

...and was woken by steaming hot coffee under my nose, served in a vintage EPCOT Center mug. This was nice. This I could get behind. Anyone who served coffee in a vintage EPCOT Center mug was okay by me.

"It is thirteen-hundred hours, Mr. McKinnon, and you need to wake up!" said the fat tattooed man, jumping around like Tweedledee (or Tweedledum, I guess).

How did he know my name? Oh, yeah, right, he knew it because he was my limo driver, and he must have been holding a sign with my name on it. Which I didn't see, because I was too busy puking on his shoes.

I sat up and he handed me four ibuprofen and the coffee, and laid down on the table a glass of orange juice (a picture of Orange Bird was printed on the glass) and a fancy plate of gold-leaf-rimmed china engraved with "Disney's Grand Floridian Resort & Spa" on the edge. On the china were two Mickey-shaped waffles, two slices of bacon, and some scrambled eggs. I threw the pills into my mouth, followed by a gulp of the OJ and a gulp of the coffee, which burned my tongue. Which was fine.

"You're a lifesaver, uh, Disney Tattoo Guy."

He looked at me, amused. "Yes, I will answer to 'Disney Tattoo Guy' at the parks, but here at home I go by Jay."

"Ah, okay, cool. Jay.... Jay the Disney Tattoo Guy." I said, mulling it over in my head. A picture from somewhere on the Internet flashed into my head. It was him! "Yeah, yeah! You're the Disney Tattoo Guy! I've seen pictures of you on the Internet! You're famous!"

Jay looked happy about being recognized. "I am pretty famous. Some people call me a living legend." He turned his head down, a strange look on his face. "That's taking it a bit far, but yes, I am a local celebrity, which has its perks."

I was feeling slightly more normal. This guy was hilarious. Everything was cool. Except, I still didn't know how I'd got there.

"Jay, if I may ask the question of the day... why am I not in my room at The Beach Club? Why am I sleeping on your couch instead of in my posh resort bed?"

He answered slowly, like I was a complete idiot. "Because you were falling down drunk and vomiting and urinating all over everything, and if you'd tried to check into your room in that condition, you would've been banned from the hotel, and likely the entire resort."

"Ah... yep, that's true. That's very true."

This man, this extremely unusual fat man with a nicely trimmed moustache and a lot of Disney tattoos, had saved me from being banned from the place I came here to visit. The place that would heal me. If I'd been banned on my first night.... Well, that would not have been a good scene. I wasn't sure how to express my gratitude.

"So, yeah, thank you for thinking of that. I really owe you one... or three or ten."

I started shoveling down the eggs. A whole piece of bacon disappeared down my throat, washed down with a gulp of coffee. I grabbed for one of the Mickey waffles. I bit its left ear off.

Jay laughed. "Everyone always goes for the ears first!"

I laughed, too. This guy was okay.

5

—I awoke from another nap, feeling much better. The headache was mostly gone, although the back of my eyes still felt weird. My mouth was dry. My kidneys ached. But other than that, I was doing okay.

"Jay, could I get a glass of water?" I called to nowhere in particular.

No answer.

"Jay? Water?" I said a little louder.

Nothing. He obviously wasn't in the house.

I stood up and put on my vintage EPCOT Center t-shirt, which was laid out on the mirror table, completely stain-free.

"Kick ass," I said to myself. So far, absolutely no negative ramifications from my day of debauchery. Maybe I was being a bit extreme saying I'd never drink again....

There was a note pinned to the bottom of the shirt.

"Gone to pick up the limo," it read. "Be back by 16:00 to drive you to The Beach Club. – Jay"

Awesome. I'd soon be at The Beach Club, where I could finally start my real "vacation", or whatever the fuck it was that I was doing here in Florida.

But right now, I needed a drink of water. I stumbled around the mirror table and changed my mind – no, what I needed first was to shit. Badly. I hobbled forward, saw the kitchen, turned around, walked a step, turned again, walked another step, and stopped, realizing I had no idea where the bathroom was. Spying a carpeted hallway, I bolted, flinging open every door before finally catching a glimpse of a Mickey Mouse shower curtain.

My pants were down before I'd crossed the threshold, and in a split second the remnants of whatever had been left in my stomach after yesterday's puke-athon spewed out of my ass with extreme force.

"Ahhh…" I sighed.

After washing my hands with soap shaped like Mickey which I found in a Little Mermaid-sitting-on-a-seashell soap dish, and wiping them on a towel embroidered with Tinker Bell, I cracked the window and pulled a Lightning McQueen cup from a badass Pooh's hunny pot dispenser. I filled the cup with water, downed the contents, and repeated about eighty times. Much better.

Walking back towards the living room, I realized that I'd opened every single door in his main hallway. Obviously this had to be rectified, but not before I'd peeked into each room. Every one was filled with an astounding amount of Disney crap. Just a massive collection of trinkets, dolls, lunch boxes, statuettes, Mouse Ears, music boxes, records, books…. It was like a fucking museum! I had no idea whether it was all a bunch of junk, and Jay was a crazy pack-rat, or if everything was ultra-rare and collectible, making Jay a shrewd millionaire. Either way, the dude had a hardcore Disney obsession.

As I was closing the door of the last room I caught sight of a really old-looking metal contraption on a stand, rust and peeling white paint covering it, with a crank on the front and some sort of viewfinder on the top. I couldn't resist. I walked into the room and up to the device, which said "Mutoscope" on the inner ring of the viewfinder. I looked into the viewfinder, turned the crank, and the screen filled with light as photos on a reel flipped past fast enough to turn them into a movie of W.C. Fields playing golf. It was just like the little cartoon flip-books I used to draw as a kid! Now this, this had to be worth something.

I tore my eyes away from the viewfinder and examined the

exterior, wondering what the hell it had to do with Disney. Attached to the top was a little frame that presumably held a title card for the movie. But in the frame was a wide shot of Jay with one arm around this very machine, the other around a young girl by his side, standing inside a wide, ornate entryway. Above the entrance was a sign that read "Penny Arcade". I recognized it immediately as being from Main Street at The Magic Kingdom. The Penny Arcade had been long since replaced with a regular store that sold standard Disney merchandise, which was complete bullshit.

I wondered who the girl was… a daughter, maybe?

I turned and scanned the room. On top of a table that looked like it'd been made from fake tree trunks, and was likely a discard from Frontierland, sat a photo album. I looked around. Should I open the photo album? Was I this big of a snoop? Did I really want to risk getting caught red-handed?

Yep.

The album flew open. Young and skinny Jay with a wife and one kid, no tattoos, at The Magic Kingdom. Pages turned. Two kids, same wife, slightly fatter Jay, still with no tattoos, at EPCOT Center. He looks miserable. Jumped ahead a few more pages. A newspaper clipping. "Drifter Arrested for Attempted Convenience Store Robbery" shouts the headline. A picture of a man from the back, a Snow White tattoo on his shoulder. We can't see his face, but who the hell else can it be? Turned to the next page. "Drifter Sentenced to Ten Years in Jail". Damn. Next page. Jay, a totally different kid, totally different wife, at MGM Studios. Jay's shoulders covered in tattoos. Flipped through just a few more pages. No wife, same kid, older, maybe twelve, Jay, kinda fat, both arms covered in tattoos, at Animal Kingdom, in front of some big tree thing. Turned the page. Nothing. Empty.

I slammed the book shut.

What. The. Fuck.

I hightailed it out of the room and jumped back onto the couch, covered myself with the *Lion King* blanket, and spent thirty minutes trying to sort out the timeline in the photo album, before

Jay finally came back.

"How're you feeling, champ?" he asked, even more chipper than before. "The stains all came out of your shirt!"

"Yeah, man, that's awesome. Thanks so much for that. I'm feeling good. Almost normal."

"Even better," he said, "the urine smell came out of my upholstery!"

"Thank God for that!" I said.

I digested his cherubic expression like an antacid. It quelled the sickening feeling I'd had since looking at the photo album. It felt like a fist pushing into my gut, telling me that maybe something was off here. But his sweet, innocent, glee-filled expression stopped that fist cold, and I guess I felt like everything was going to be okay.

How did he do that? How did he make people feel that way with just a smile?

6

—We drove to The Beach Club in Jay's limo, which, even if the piss smell was gone, still stunk like vomit. I felt bad about that, but not bad enough to stop myself from pouring a gin and tonic from the limo's bar.

Jay looked back over the divider. "Watch yourself," he said. "We don't want a repeat of yesterday."

"Hair of the dog, Jay. I'll be fine." I pushed the button to make the divider go up. Jay pushed a button on his console to make it go back down. I sighed and looked out the window, nursing my gin and tonic.

We turned right at a light, and passed a Hess gas station. "Just like the one down the street from my house in Baltimore," I thought. This immediately brought forth into the periphery of my mind's eye an image of my backyard, which I apparently couldn't picture anymore without seeing Sam, bloody, hanging from his tree.

I was going to have to sell that house. I never wanted to go back there again.

I shut out the memory of Sam with a gulp of my drink and tried to concentrate on the scenery.

On the left I saw a large, white, ornate sign for The BoardWalk Inn, another Disney resort with a 1920s Coney Island theme. I knew we were close to our destination, because according to the Fodor's guide I'd bought at the airport and skimmed before getting completely obliterated in the plane, The BoardWalk overlooks Crescent Lake, along with The Yacht Club, The Beach Club, and The Swan and Dolphin. I fully intended to spend many hours lounging on the white beach surrounding the lake, taking in the sun, sipping a drink with an umbrella in it, and not giving two fucks about shit like selling my house.

"On the right is Epcot's backstage area," said Jay, pointing. "That's the back of the France pavilion right there."

I saw a fence and some trees. "Fascinating, Jay," I responded, sarcastically.

He continued, unfazed. "And right now we're about to go under a canal that the Friendship Boats sail in. They carry people between the resorts and Epcot's International Gateway."

Sure enough, we drove underneath what appeared to be a regular overpass. "Really? We just went under a canal with boats in it?" I asked, genuinely surprised.

"Yes, we did!"

"Cool," I said, turning to gawk at the overpass through the rear window.

It disappeared as we rounded a corner. I whipped around and caught my first glimpse of the place I'd be staying for the foreseeable future: The Beach Club. One half of what is traditionally called "The Yacht and Beach Club", because of its proximity and similarity in theme to The Yacht Club next door. The Beach Club nonetheless has its own thing going on. Modeled after Cape Cod vacation homes, it's painted soft blue and sea-foam green, with white trim and shutters. The buildings stretch and wind around a drainage ditch made to look like a relaxing canal, with white bridges crossing it at various points. I'd come to find that there were turtles living in that canal, dozens of them, and that they'd come out every afternoon when the sun was high and bob towards the top of the water. Every time I'd cross the bridges I'd look out for those turtles, and if I saw them I'd always stop and stare for a while. I'm not sure why I liked them so much….

As we drove up to the lobby I remembered walking through

the resort with my parents, marveling at the décor, knowing that we weren't nearly wealthy enough to stay here but wanting to experience as much of it as we could. A wave of sadness and remorse hit me as I desperately wished they could be here to stay in my fancy suite. Seeing their faces when they realized they would finally be staying in the place that was always so far out of their reach financially maybe would have made all the years of building up my wealth not seem like such a fucking waste of time.

I wiped a tear away and tried to smile. Now wasn't the time to dredge this shit up.

The limo stopped under an ornate overhang and Jay stepped out, walked to the side of the car, and opened the door.

We were immediately accosted by an extremely well dressed, extremely agitated older black gentleman. He looked like he'd just stepped off the fucking *Love Boat*. Crisp white slacks, a blue coat festooned with gold buttons and gold trim on the shoulders, spotless white gloves, and a white and black captain's hat covering short gray hair. His nametag read "Charles" and below that "Nashville, TN".

Jay moved next to me and pushed me back a bit.

"You get right the hell on out of here, you son of a bitch!" Charles said forcefully, but not loud enough for anyone except for me and Jay to hear.

"Uh, I have a reservation for a concierge suite?" I said, hoping that would calm him down.

"Not you. Him!" He shoved a finger into Jay's chest, hard. Jay winced, but took it.

"Calm down, Charles," said Jay. "I'm just here to drop off Mr. McKinnon."

"You son of a bitch. You goddamned son of a bitch. That's bullshit! You're here to push me, to push me straight over the edge. Well, I won't let you!"

Charles turned to me. "Is he selling to you, son? You better not be bringing that shit into my place of work!"

"No! I mean… what?" I looked at Jay. "What the hell, Jay?"

One of the Cast Members from the valet stand slowly approached. "Is there a problem, Charles?"

Jay answered, looking at Charles. "No problem." He turned to the valet. "If you could give me a hand with Mr. McKinnon's luggage I'll be on my way."

The Cast Member looked at Charles. "Uh, so can you please show Mr. McKinnon to the lobby, Charles?"

Charles broke his death-ray stare-down with Jay, looked at me, looked at the luggage, looked at the valet, and changed his expression entirely.

"Of course I can!" he beamed, his bright white teeth matching his bright white gloves. And then with more zest and kindness in his voice than I'd heard from anyone in a long time, he nearly shouted, "Welcome to The Beach Club, sir! Concierge check-in is at The Stone Harbor Club on the fifth floor. Let me bring you there!"

I followed Charles to the front door of the hotel, looking back at Jay with a "what the fuck?" expression. Jay made the universal signal for "call me" and continued to help the valet unload my myriad assortment of heavy bags.

Charles whisked me into the lobby, which was spacious and bright and pastel-colored, and filled with comfy-looking couches and wicker chairs. I loved it.

We reached an elevator and stepped in. Charles pulled a key out of his pocket, which he inserted into a red lock near the top of the elevator's control panel. He put a plastic keycard into a slot above the "five" button and pressed the button for the fifth floor. The button lit up, the door closed, and we started moving. But then he turned the key in the red lock and the elevator stopped. He turned to face me.

"Son, I'm gonna give you the benefit of the doubt here. I'm gonna try real hard to believe that you didn't know the kind of man you were associating with back there. Because if I you're anything like him, you and I are gonna have some problems."

"Charles, I honestly have no idea what you're talking about. Jay has been nothing but nice to me."

"That's how he gets you! That's how he draws you in!"

An alarm started going off and Charles quickly turned the key and pulled it out of the lock. The alarm stopped and the elevator lurched upwards.

"You need to stay away from that man, Mr. McKinnon. He is nothing but pure evil."

We reached the fifth floor. The door opened and Charles stepped out.

"This way, sir," he said, with a comforting warmth. This attitude flip-flopping was starting to freak me out.

He led me to one of the two desks in front of The Stone Harbor Club, the concierge area of The Beach Club. Apparently they had free food and booze in there somewhere. Seriously in need of a drink, I looked around but didn't see anything resembling alcohol. Fuck.

"This is Mr. McKinnon," Charles told the semi-hot Cast Member behind the desk. "He'll be checking in today."

"Thank you so much, Charles," the Cast Member said. Her nametag read "Sandra" and she was from "Charlotte, NC". There was nothing in the way she looked at Charles that indicated she thought he was totally off his fucking rocker. Weird.

"Have a magical day, sir," said Charles. "I'm in the lobby most of the time if you ever need anything." He turned and went down the elevator with nary a glance back.

Confused, I looked at Sandra, who was a bit mousy, but was definitely semi-hot. "So, uh, that Charles is quite a guy, huh?"

"Oh yes, sir! 'Charles the Greeter' is sort of a living legend among visitors to The Beach Club. Many people stay here just because of him!"

"Seriously?"

"I've never met a nicer man in my whole life," said Sandra. She started typing.

"I'll be damned."

Semi-Hot Sandra continued to type. She stopped and looked

dumbfounded at the screen.

"Is there a problem?" I asked.

"Well, it's just that there's no check-out date here. That can't be right."

"No, no, it's right. I don't know when I'm checking out. I'll be here a while."

"Unfortunately, our system won't let you check in without a check-out date." She typed some more and clicked the mouse a few times. "So...." She looked up at me and smiled in a way that I interpreted as being at least a little flirtatious. "It seems like we'll be seeing each other on a regular basis."

"Huh?"

"I promise you'll always have the same room, but I'm going to need you to come back here every two weeks and run through the check-out, check-in process. I'll add this as a note on your account, so even if I'm not here I can assure you that the process will be quick and smooth."

I sighed, and then smiled. "Be charming, asshole," I thought to myself.

"Well," I said, "I guess there are worse things than having to talk to an attractive girl every two weeks."

She blushed, embarrassed.

"And," I continued, playing interference after obviously not receiving the reaction I'd hoped for, which I guess was for her to jump me right then and there, "I hear there's booze in this place somewhere? That'll keep me coming back more than once every two weeks, for sure."

"Yes, we do offer wine, beer, and cordials," said Semi-Hot Sandra, "but only from five PM to ten PM." She smiled again, and I swear there's no way she wasn't flirting with me when she said, "But if I'm at the desk I can get you anything you want, at any time."

"Anything?" I asked, winking. I immediately felt like a creep. Trying to recover, I blurted, "Um, yeah, that's mighty fine service."

Mighty fine? Had I suddenly turned into Barney Fife? What

the fuck? Man, I sucked at this.

Apparently she agreed, because she turned, stone-faced, looked at the computer, typed a bit more and handed me my light blue keycard with a picture of Cinderella Castle on it.

"You're in the Nantucket Suite, room 5691. Just go straight down the hall, take your first left, and then take the another left."

"Thanks," I said, taking the key.

"Your luggage should arrive shortly." She looked at the clock, "And you're in luck, because we'll be setting out some snacks and beverages in just a few minutes!"

"Cool," I said, walking out of the lounge. No way I was going back in there. I'd already done enough damage with this girl. Getting drunk in front of her was not going to help the situation.

"I think I'm going straight to The Magic Kingdom," I lied. "See you in two weeks!"

I walked down the hall to my room, opened the door with the key, and was pretty blown away by the size of the place. Granted, for nearly $900 a night, I'm not sure what I was expecting, but it was impressive. There was a huge living room with two sliding glass doors that opened up onto balconies which overlooked the lake outside, as well as The BoardWalk across the way. On the right was a wet bar and a half-bathroom, and then a sofa facing an armoire with a TV in it, next to which was a small dinette with a window that also looked out onto the lake. The entrance to my bedroom was on the right, too, before the sofa. I walked in and was happy at how bright and cozy it was. A big bed, another TV, a lounging sofa, and a balcony. On the right was the bathroom, which was done up in what looked like dark marble. Two sinks (with a little TV in between), the shitter in its own little room, a shower, and a Jacuzzi tub, which no doubt was going to get a lot of use.

I pictured sitting in the Jacuzzi tub, watching The Disney Channel nonstop on the little TV, and sipping port or some shit like that. The idea of being able to relax, to do something like sitting in a bathtub all day, was really exciting. Was that sort of thing exciting to everyone? I had no idea. Man, I was out of touch, almost like I wasn't even part of the human race anymore. I simply had no idea how normal people lived, or thought, or felt.

So, I figured, why not go where the people were? I nearly sprinted out of the room, excited to see EPCOT Center, and most of all Horizons.

7

—The walk from The Beach Club to EPCOT Center was fairly pleasant. I still remembered the route, and walked casually through the exit past the gift store, hung a right, and hung another right to end up on a trail that bordered what seemed to be swampland. There was a slight drop-off next to the sidewalk, into dense foliage that smelled vaguely of sulfur. I could hear things scurrying around down there, and saw some little lizards running across the path into the brush. Ah, Florida!

The trail dumped out onto a wide pathway facing Crescent Lake. Ahead of me was The BoardWalk, on the right was The Swan and Dolphin, and on the left I spied The Eiffel Tower, not anywhere near scale, sticking out of the France pavilion in EPCOT Center.

I bolted left to what's known as the International Gateway, which was sort of the back entrance to EPCOT Center. I reached the ticket booth in no time flat. I didn't notice the signage and logos that clearly stated this place was now called Epcot, not EPCOT Center.

"One Annual Pass, please," I said to the old lady in the booth.

"Would you like the regular Annual Pass, or the Premium Annual Pass?" she asked.

"Beats me. What's the price difference?"

"Well now, that depends," she said. "Are you a Florida resident?"

"Not yet!"

"Okay, then. A regular will be four hundred and fifty two dollars."

"Christ, almighty."

"And the Premium is an additional one hundred and twenty dollars, which gives you unlimited access to our virtual theme park, DisneyQuest, as well as unlimited access to our amazing water parks, Typhoon Lagoon and Blizzard Beach."

"Okay, sure, fine. I don't know what most of that stuff is, but whatever. Sold." I paused as memories of going down water slides that winded through fake sculpted rocks near Bay Lake entered my mind. "Wait. You only mentioned two water parks. What happened to River Country?"

"River Country has been closed for ages, sir."

"That sucks. I liked that place. My parents and I used to go there a lot."

"I'm sure you'll enjoy the other water parks just as much. They're very well themed!"

I handed her my credit card and after a few minutes she handed me back a silver piece of plastic.

"The gate is on your left. Enjoy your year of magic!" she exclaimed.

I walked toward the gate, straight through the bag inspection area, which seemed a bit out of place at "The Happiest Place on Earth", chose the turnstile on the far left, slid my card in the slot, and pushed at the turnstile. It didn't move.

"Sir, you have to scan your finger," explained the gate attendant.

"What are you talking about?" I asked.

"Your finger. You have to put it on this pad. It'll scan your finger so that you will be linked to that Annual Pass."

I stared at it. Interesting technology. Biometric scanner. Didn't actually store the fingerprint, just the spacing between the tip of the finger and the first joint. I put my pass through, put my finger on the scanner, the turnstile clicked, and I walked through.

"Have a magical day!" the gate attendant chimed.

"Uh huh," I replied. Between the fucking bag check and the

biometric scanner it didn't seem like a very "magical" way to start your day. They didn't have any of that shit when I'd been there last. A foreboding feeling passed over me. What else had changed since my last visit?

I literally ran past the United Kingdom and Canada pavilions. So far everything looked the same... until I hit the rose-filled path that linked Future World and World Showcase, which offered me my first unfettered glimpse at the main icon of EPCOT Center: Spaceship Earth. A massive triumph of architecture, it's an eighteen-story geodesic sphere, the only one in existence. The scale of the structure is massive and awe-inspiring... under normal circumstances. Except now, when I looked at it I couldn't believe what I was seeing.

There was a huge wand stuck onto the side of the globe.

Mickey's hand was holding the wand, and there were little red stars everywhere. "Epcot" was written above it in an ugly, decidedly non-futuristic font. It completely diminished the magnitude and majesty of the structure, demeaning it and reducing it to a placeholder for a prop, essentially saying "Mickey's hand is way bigger than this insignificant building. Mickey is master of all."

Something was very wrong here.

That foreboding feeling I'd felt at the gate became exponentially worse. I ran east to Horizons faster than I could remember running since I was a kid. Just past the breezeway between the Stargate Restaurant (now called Electric Umbrella – WTF did that mean?) and the Centorium gift shop (now called Mouse Gear – which, while clever, had no futuristic connotations whatsoever) was the first clear view of my favorite pavilion.

Except it wasn't there.

Horizons was simply no longer there.

I knew EPCOT Center like the back of my hand. I could navigate the park blindfolded. There was no doubt that this was where Horizons should be. I continued walking towards it. I looked to the left: Wonders of Life and Universe of Energy were there, as expected. I looked to the right. What the fuck was that? It looked vaguely like World of Motion, except there were awnings all over it, and a car zoomed around a track that wrapped around the previously elegant building.

Turning forward, it finally hit me. Horizons had been demolished. And in its place was some monstrosity called Mission: SPACE.

The ride that my parents and I loved so much was gone.

For a moment, the pain of their death hit me all over again. That pain I'd stashed away and hidden deep. My throat tightened and I choked back bile.

I'd counted on Horizons being there! I'd needed it to be there, so I could ride it over and over again, comforting me and somehow finally easing me through the death of my parents. But instead, something I'd loved so much as a child, one of the few things we'd treasured together as a family, had been inexplicably destroyed. Not only had it been destroyed, but its elegance and beauty had been defiled by this atrocious thing jutting up from the ground like some evil cancerous growth. It was like someone had built a McDonald's on top of my parents' graves.

What else had been ruined here? What else had been defiled in the park I'd been counting on to be my sanctuary, my healing place?

I ran to the north. Universe of Energy still looked good. But what did the sign say? "Ellen's Energy Adventure"? As in, Ellen DeGeneres? Holy fuck. Turning around, I noticed the Wonders of Life pavilion was lifeless. I ran up the winding ramp, and was greeted with automatic doors that would not open. This was a nightmare. Down, past the repulsive Mission: SPACE, I reached World of Motion. But it was now called Test Track, and it looked like NASCAR had thrown up on it. Shit. More running, to The Odyssey, a futuristic looking building that housed a nice counter-service restaurant. The doors were locked, the lights were off. I was seriously panicking at this point. It was like an episode of *The Twilight Zone*. I stumbled to CommuniCore, but the dazzling reflecting ponds I'd remembered along the way were filled in with concrete and I got momentarily disoriented. I entered a dark building, something called Innoventions, and scrambled through a bleak maze, trying to find an exit. Then I realized I was walking through what used to be CommuniCore, Sam's favorite part of the park. Except now it was all dark and claustrophobic, and there was no sign of SMRT-1 anywhere. I started hyperventilating, and doubled over. A Cast Member came up to me.

"Are you okay?" he asked.

"How do I get out of here?" I nearly cried. "Journey into Imagination?"

He pointed to a blacked-out automatic sliding door. "That way."

I bolted through the doors, which slid open, revealing a blinding light and the Fountain of Nations. I stopped for a minute, watching the fountain show. There was an ugly wooden stage erected all around it that ruined its elegantly sculpted foundation, but at least the fountain itself was still there, shooting water into the sky in sync with music. But then I turned to the right and saw that fucking wand on Spaceship Earth, and it freaked me out. I didn't even want to look at it, much less ride it. I started running again, towards Imagination.

It was still there. The Imagination pavilion looked just about the same. Sure, the bottom half had a gaudy paint job, but at least it was still standing. I walked inside, expecting the vast open airy expanse I remembered, and instead was greeted with a cheap ass plywood queue. There was literally nobody in the line, so I shot straight through the queue and hopped on the vehicle. It moved into a darkened tunnel and Eric Idle popped up.

What the hell was Monty Python doing in EPCOT Center? Where was Dreamfinder, the jolly bearded host of the ride?

Well, at least Figment, the little purple dragon who was essentially EPCOT Center's mascot, was there. But he was being a dick, not nice and loveable like he used to be. The ride continued on, a shell of its former self. Figment farted on the audience at one point and I swear I wanted to punch somebody.

"What the hell did you do with Dreamfinder?" I asked a Cast

Member as I got off the ride.

"Dreamfinder retired years ago, after the first refurbishment of the ride!"

"Refurbishment? This was appallingly bad! How is it a refurbishment if you make it worse than it was before?"

"Many Guests have expressed their unhappiness with the ride, sir. I'd highly recommend that if you want Dreamfinder to return you fill out a complaint at Guest Services."

"Goddamned right I will. Thanks for the tip."

"No problem, sir. Have a magical day!"

"That's not going to happen. Is Image Works still upstairs?"

"No sir, it's been closed since…"

I cut him off. "Since the refurbishment? Fucking hell!"

"They did move some of the exhibits into the gift shop, right through these doors."

With two fingers he pointed towards the exit, which dumped me straight into hell. It was packed with kids, and was loud and uncomfortably cramped. Nothing like the expansive second floor Image Works. I got the hell out of there as fast as I could.

I felt beaten down. Nothing I'd loved about EPCOT Center was there anymore. It'd all been demolished or bastardized somehow. A wrinkled guidebook skittered along the ground, being dragged around by the wind. I caught it, picked it up and looked at the front. "Epcot", it said. Not "EPCOT Center". Not even "EPCOT". Nope, just "Epcot". That didn't even make sense. It wasn't supposed to be a proper noun, it was an acronym. What the fuck is an "Epcot"? Obviously the people in charge of this place didn't have any concept of what the park was supposed to be, or why it was built in the first place.

"They've ruined my favorite place on earth," I thought as I slumped down on a bench. Maybe it was best that my parents hadn't lived to see this. A tear fell down my face, and that turned into a sob, and that became one of those heaving bawling things where snot bubbles out of your nose and your mouth is all contorted and shit. People were walking by staring at me, but I couldn't help it.

I couldn't stop crying.

I was crying because my parents were dead, and because Horizons was destroyed, and because I'd always assumed like an arrogant kid that everything and everyone would be around forever.

If I'd known I'd never get to see my parents again, of course I would've spent more time with them, showed them more respect, told them I loved them more often....

Anyway, great, fine, I got it: Don't take the people and things you love for granted. Thanks for shoving important life-lessons down my throat, shitty lower-case "Epcot".

After what might have been an hour of crying, I composed myself, wiped the snot and tears from my face, stood up, and started walking again. The sun had set, and I had to admit that the park looked gorgeous. The crystalline Imagination building was lit a vibrant purple, and the fountain in front was glowing orange, and just then the monorail silently glided past, and it was all quite enchanting and very much like I'd remembered it. In keeping with my newly minted "don't take shit for granted" outlook on life, I decided that even if the rides were fucked up and stuff was flat out gone, there were at least some things here I could still enjoy. I walked slowly towards The Land, taking in the atmosphere. The music piped in from hidden speakers was the same loop they'd always played, themes I must have somehow subconsciously stowed away, because I found myself humming along with every track.

Walking into The Land I was blasted with a mouth-watering smell unique to food courts: spices and ingredients from all sorts of different cuisines mixed together into one whomping blast of olfactory goodness. I remembered I hadn't eaten since my post-hangover breakfast that morning and was hungry as all fuck as a result. Thank God they obviously hadn't torn out the kick ass food court on the first floor. My eyes were bigger than my stomach as I walked through the various food stations. I grabbed a ham panini, a bowl of Japanese noodles and tofu, a Caesar salad, and a

Heineken.

Sitting down, I started stuffing my face, barely pausing to breath. I nearly got through all the food, too, with only bits of the noodles and some bread from the panini left over. I washed it down with a final gulp of beer and started looking around.

On my left was a big sign that said "Soarin'". I didn't know what the hell Soarin' was, but the name alone bugged me because it was missing a "g", not to mention the fact that they'd apparently torn out Kitchen Kabaret to build it. Under the sign lay a queue that looked like an airport terminal. I was just in an airport two days ago. Looking at the queue made me feel like I was back there again, like my vacation was already over and I had to go back home. It stressed me out. Soarin' could go fuck itself.

On my right, however, was Living with the Land, which by all appearances was the same boat ride through animatronic-filled landscapes and an honest-to-god futuristic greenhouse that I remembered loving as a kid. Could this finally be an untouched piece of EPCOT Center? Once again, there was no line at all for the ride, so I ran onto the boat, waved at the attendant, and beamed as the boat floated down an artificial canal into a rainforest. The spiel in the greenhouse was now prerecorded and no longer narrated by a real human being standing there in the boat, but whatever. It was a minor change, especially considering everything else was just as I'd remembered. When the ride ended I asked the attendant if I could stay on the boat and ride it through again. And for good measure, I rode it once more after that. I was kinda happy now.

Exiting The Land, I looked to the north and saw that The Living Seas now had *Finding Nemo* characters splattered all over it, so I immediately turned around and went the other direction, through what used to be CommuniCore West. There was a large indoor breezeway here that looked like it was straight out of 1982, like the people who'd fucked this place up somehow forgot the hallway existed. I sat on one of the benches in there for a while and looked up at the huge domed faux skylights above. Awesome.

I felt relaxed as I walked through the non-blacked-out sliding doors at the end of the breezeway and saw the Fountain of Nations all lit up, once again blowing water into the air in sync with a soundtrack. I looked to my left and noticed that from this angle I really couldn't see the wand on Spaceship Earth. It occurred to me that maybe if I stayed on this side of it I'd be able to walk up to the ride without wanting to vomit. I was glad I did, because the ride itself was just as awesome as it'd always been, except that Jeremy Irons was doing the narration instead of Walter Cronkite. My first reaction was annoyance and I kinda wanted to tell Jeremy Irons to shut up, but then I decided it could have been worse: at least he was taking the ride seriously. It could have been Gilbert Gottfried cracking fart jokes or something like that. I rode Spaceship Earth three times, too.

After I exited the ride, now devoid of the old post-show, I took the Imagination Cast Member's advice and filled out a complaint form at Guest Services. But I also wrote on there the stuff that I really enjoyed, just so it wasn't all negative whining.

I was surprised to get a call from a lady a few weeks later who wanted to talk to me about why I hated Imagination so much. I tried to explain to her that they'd ruined a wonderful ride, but she wasn't getting it, so I jumped onto YouTube, found a ride-thru video of the original version, read the link to her, and made her watch it while I stayed on the phone with her. At the end of the video there was silence.

"So, what'd you think?" I asked.

"That was amazing," she said.

"I know. That's why it's sad that you guys fucked it up."

"I'm sorry we've disappointed you, Mr. McKinnon."

"Your condolences are appreciated. Please tell your superiors I'd be glad to offer my consultation the next time they decide to 'refurbish' one of your classic rides."

"I'll do that, Mr. McKinnon. Thank you for your time, and have a magical day."

Later that year a temporary EPCOT Center museum opened

up in my untouched 80s CommuniCore breezeway, in celebration of the park's 25th Anniversary. It had props from all of the opening-day pavilions, and whoever put it together obviously had a deep appreciation for the original vision of the park. That sorta gave me hope for the future of EPCOT Center. (I still refuse to call it "Epcot").

8

—I legit did spend that evening in my Jacuzzi, sipping port and watching The Disney Channel. Or at least, I watched The Disney Channel for a few minutes and then changed it because the shows were annoying and they weren't playing any of the classic Walt stuff. I flipped through the stations until I came across the Resort Channel, which showed a thirty minute loop of some chick named Tracey running around the parks, riding the rides and hyping up various parts of Walt Disney World. It was pretty entertaining, so I watched that for a while and then rubbed one out because she was hot.

Anyway, it was a relaxing evening is my point.

The next day I spent sitting on a lounge chair on the beach, reading a book about The Imagineers that I'd purchased at The Art of Disney store in EPCOT Center. In between chapters I drank various brightly colored tropical drinks, watched the Friendship Boats go back and forth between the hotels, EPCOT Center, and Disney-MGM Studios, and watched moms and their jailbait daughters in bikinis walking between the hotels and Stormalong Bay, the Yacht and Beach Club's waterpark area.

As I was coming back from the "beach" I ran into "Charles the Greeter" in the lobby.

"Hey, Charles," I said, walking briskly to the elevator to avoid getting into a confrontation with him.

"Hello, good sir," he said, showing me a large portion of his bright white teeth. "You and I should have a cocktail together some evening soon."

"You bet, Charles. I'd love that."

"How about Thursday evening? Thursday's my day off! Let's meet in the Belle Vue Lounge in the second floor of The BoardWalk Inn at eight PM. I'm buying!"

"Um, okay, sure. Thursday at eight PM at the Belle Vue. I'll be there."

"Looking forward to it, Mr. McKinnon!"

Shit. What had I gotten myself into?

I walked back to the room and tried to forget all about "Charles the Greeter". I sat in the Jacuzzi, and watched Tracey going down the slides at the water parks, and once again rubbed one out.

My one-sided relationship with Tracey couldn't continue forever, though. I decided I probably needed to try to meet a real girl, or at the very least start socializing with people. So, as tempting as it was to sit on the beach watching jailbait again the next day, and then come home to masturbate to a water-sliding Tracey, I decided to get my ass in gear and visit The Magic Kingdom. It was crazy that I'd been in Florida for three days and still hadn't set foot inside the park that had made Orlando a vacation destination.

Instead of taking a bus over, I walked through EPCOT Center and hopped on the monorail outside the front gate. I had a cab all to myself, so I swung on the overhead grab rails like they were monkey bars, just because I could. The monorail disembarked at the Transportation and Ticket Center, where I then had the choice to take either a ferry or another monorail over to the park entrance. I decided to do the ferry, since I wanted to get the full Seven Seas Lagoon experience.

At the gate my Annual Pass worked as expected, and I went through the turnstile, into the tunnel under the railroad station, and out into expanse of Main Street. Something about that first view immediately brought back a feeling of childhood excitement, and I savored the memory of seeing it that first time with my parents and grandparents. I wasted no time getting into the meat of the park, starting at Adventureland and winding my way around to Tomorrowland, riding all of my favorite rides, happy that the place was pretty much the same as the last time I was there, aside from a fairly ugly facelift to Tomorrowland. I even bought a pair of Haunted Mansion-themed Mouse Ears, which I wore with pride. It was a fun day, and I pretty much had a big dumb grin on my face the whole time. I really was starting to feel like a kid again.

As I was leaving, I saw a group of people clustered around an alcove in Town Square, so I walked over to see what all the hubbub was about. I wormed my way through the crowd, knocking over a little girl in the process, but didn't really feel bad about it because she was fat and not at all cute. But then I felt bad about not feeling bad about it so I gave her twenty bucks. Which she'd probably just spend on candy. Because she was fat.

I finally got to the front of the crowd and saw Snow White sitting with some snot-nosed kid. My first reaction was, "Aw, shit, this is a waste of time," but then that disease-factory of a kid got off her lap and I looked closely at her and I swear I fell in love.

Like, seriously, right then and there I think I fell in love with Snow White.

Even through all the makeup and the stupid costume and the screaming kids climbing on her, I was dumbstruck by how gorgeous she was. There was something about her eyes, and the way she was looking at the kids, and the way she was handling herself that wasn't quite princess-esque, but almost goth or punk or something. I didn't know what it was, but this Snow White had attitude, and it was hot.

So, I decided to get my picture taken with her. Yep, I was going to sit next to her and get my picture taken. I cut in front of a few kids who were too busy staring at their shoes or some dumb shit like that and in a few minutes I was at the front of the line.

"And what is your child's name?" asked the Cast Member gatekeeper.

"What child? I don't have a child. It's just me. I want to get my picture taken with Snow White. Is that a problem?"

"Absolutely not, sir. Just please be respectful of the princess. Inappropriate behavior will not be tolerated."

"Dude, it's not like I'm going to grab her tits or anything. I just want a picture with her…."

He stammered as I handed him my camera and walked over to Snow White.

I sat on the bench next to her. It was a small bench and we were pressed closely together. She smelled like makeup.

"Oh, what wonderful Mouse Ears!" she exclaimed.

I'd forgotten I was wearing them. I must have looked like the biggest dork.

"What's your name, my charming prince?" she lilted. Her voice was kinda annoying, actually. It was high-pitched and nasally.

"Uh, it's Blaine. Look, you don't have to do all of the character bullshit. I just thought you were really beautiful and I wanted a picture of us together. Which, now that I'm saying it out loud, sounds pretty fucking creepy. Shit. Sorry."

I started to stand up, but she pulled me back down to the bench.

"You're not so bad yourself," she said in a low, husky, extraordinarily sensual voice.

"Oh, damn!" I said quietly, immediately popping a major boner.

"Now turn around and let's take this picture, okay?"

"Yes, ma'am!"

The Cast Member snapped the picture, and I stood up and turned to Snow White, my obvious erection pointing straight at her face. She looked right at it, smiled seductively, spun me around, and lightly pushed me towards the frowning photographer.

"Shame on you," he said, as he looked down at my pants and then handed me my camera. "Think of the children!"

"It's not my fault she's so fucking hot," I said.

As I walked towards the exit I heard someone calling my name. "Blaine, over here! It's Jay!"

Holy shit, it really was Jay! He was wearing a sleeveless shirt that showed off his tattoos. The shirt was tucked into jean shorts. Classy. Kids were staring and pointing, and a few were actually touching the tattoos. He seemed to enjoy the attention.

I walked over to him and we shook hands.

"What are you doing, stalking Snow White or something?" I joked. "I mean, I can't say I'd blame you or anything."

He grinned as my mouth kept flapping. "She is so hot, I can't believe it. Have you ever seen a princess that hot? I wonder what she looks like without all that makeup? I wonder what she looks like under that dress! Huh? Yeah? You know what I'm talking about?!"

"Blaine, that's my girlfriend," deadpanned Jay, with a Mona Lisa smile.

"Ha, yeah, right, in your dreams, maybe!"

"No, seriously, Blaine, that's Lisa. She's my girlfriend. That's why I'm standing here."

My jaw hit the fucking floor. I looked at his fat gut, his bald head, and his appalling fashion sense. No fucking way this dude was dating Snow White.

"No fucking way you're dating Snow White," I said.

He chuckled and shook his head. "Look, stick around for a bit and I'll take you down to the Utilidors. Lisa's shift ends in a few minutes. We can grab a snack at the employee cafeteria while she gets out of costume and takes her makeup off."

"Seriously?"

"Yeah, seriously. I have free reign of this place, and mi casa es su casa. I'm also having a bunch of people over for dinner tonight who I think you'd be interested in meeting."

"Um, yeah, sure, absolutely, I'd be honored!" I stammered. "Sorry I was talking like that about your girlfriend."

"Don't apologize. You're right, she is extraordinarily hot, and I have no idea how I snagged her. I'm not an idiot, Blaine." He turned and stared at Lisa as she kissed a little girl on the cheek, leaving a lipstick mark. "She's way out of my league."

"Dude," I said, watching all of the kids' dads drooling over her, "she's way out of everyone's league. You must have some serious mojo… or a monstrously huge dick."

He looked down at his crotch and back up at me. "It's gotta be mojo," he said.

We both burst out laughing and walked away from the crowd.

9

—The Utilidors are a series of huge tunnels underneath The Magic Kingdom where all the behind-the-scenes real world stuff takes place. Or, to be more specific, The Magic Kingdom was built on top of the Utilidors. They're actually at ground level, and the park is the "second floor", so to speak. They house Costuming, trash collecting, an employee bank, various kitchens for the restaurants above, employee break rooms, and two cafeterias. But perhaps more importantly, they're a way for employees to get from one part of the park to another without having to roam around in front of the Guests. It wouldn't look very good for a Cast Member dressed in Frontierland chaps to be walking across Tomorrowland in order to get to the employee parking lot. "Bad show", as they say. Instead, the Cast Member just hops into one of the myriad of hidden Utilidor entrances within the park, goes down one flight, changes into civvies, and walks through the tunnels to the exit that leads to the parking lot. These inner-workings are invisible to Guests so that the "magic" theming of the park is never disturbed.

Jay and I entered the Utilidors through a door on the northwest side of Cinderella Castle. He opened the unmarked and unremarkable door and we both stepped inside to a harshly lit dirty room filled with strollers.

"What a shithole," I said.

"I agree. Apparently the cleaning crew doesn't maintain this area."

We went down a full flight of steps and reached another door, next to which was posted an asbestos warning.

"Asbestos?" I asked, surprised that Disney would allow such a thing to exist in their wonderland.

"They treat their employees, er, Cast Members, a lot differently than they treat their Guests. I guess they're not going to do anything about the asbestos down here, and they figure a warning will suffice, at least legally."

"That's not cool."

"No, it's not. But they're a giant corporation, and they can get away with that sort of nonsense. I'm sure Lisa will be more than happy to tell you all sorts of horror stories about how the Cast Members are mistreated."

We walked down a small hallway which opened into a massive tunnel. It was filled with pipes, speeding golf carts, costumed characters, and plain-clothed off-duty Cast Members. There was peculiar mix of somewhat Disney-themed 80s hits blaring through the overhead speakers. *Mainstreet* by Bob Seger was playing as we entered the cavernous Utilidors.

"It smells disgusting down here, Jay," I said, wrinkling my nose.

"That's the trash collection," he said. "All of the trash from all of the trashcans in the park comes down here through a series of vacuum tubes." He pointed up at the pipes. "This time of year it's not so terrible. But wait until the summer comes around. The stench is overwhelming!"

"And the employee cafeteria is down here? Lovely."

"Yeah, it's just over this way."

We walked a bit and were almost run down by a few golf carts zooming around. I noticed a lot of people in regular clothes going past us.

"So anybody is allowed down here?" I asked.

"No, no, definitely not," responded Jay. "These people are all Cast Members. Not that it ever happens, but if Security thinks you look suspicious, they'll ask for your Cast Member ID. And if you don't have it and can't prove you work here, you will be thrown out of the park and possibly trespassed and BOLO'd."

"What is 'BOLO'd'?"

"'Be on the look-out for'. It means they'll take your picture and put it up everywhere, and if someone sees you in the park you'll be arrested for trespassing."

"Oh." I thought for a second. "Wait a minute, what the hell are you doing down here, then? You're not a Cast Member."

"Dating the hottest princess on property does have its advantages," said Jay. "But honestly, I've been friends with a lot of people here for years. Some of them started in janitorial and have since moved up to management. I do them favors, and they do me favors, like letting me into the parks for free and letting me roam around wherever I want."

"What kind of favors do you do for them?"

"I... procure things for them."

Just as I was about to press him for more details, we stopped at Mouseketeria. It was pretty nice, but the best part was that it was filled with Cast Members in their uniforms, all eating and talking together. It was funny seeing Captain Jack talking to a headless Mickey, who was actually a forty-something lady.

"The food here is the same stuff you'd get upstairs," said Jay as we got into line. "Except it's half as cheap. I love this place."

I ordered a soft pretzel and a soda, and Jay got some fries and a bottled water. I paid for both of us. Jay was right, it was dirt cheap. We took our food and sat down.

"So," started Jay, "you think you can come over for dinner this evening?"

"Yeah, I've got absolutely nothing planned tonight. Tomorrow I'm supposed to be having cocktails with your buddy 'Charles the Greeter', but other than that my schedule is wide open for the foreseeable future."

Jay stopped chewing. "Charles... is not the most stable person."

"No shit," I said. "Dude nearly accosted me in the elevator the other day. What's his beef with you?"

"Charles had some problems years ago, and he blames them

all on me. Needless to say, take anything he says about me with a grain of salt."

"I kinda figured. So what's his story?"

"Given his current revered status at The Beach Club, it wouldn't really be appropriate for me to reveal much. If he wants to tell you about his sordid past, that's totally up to him. But, like I said, just remember that there are two sides to every story."

"Okay, fair enough," I said. "All I know is that you've been totally cool to me since the moment we met, whereas the first time I met Charles all he did was act like a psychopath. But I can't say I'm not curious to hear what he has to tell me."

"Yes. It should be interesting."

We finished our food in silence. I started thinking about Charles's warning, and for a second had a flash of worry that maybe he was right, maybe Jay was the bad guy here. I looked up from my plate at him, and he smiled that heartwarming smile, and I just couldn't believe that this dude was anything other than a saint. And he had a really hot girlfriend that I kinda wanted to get to know better... in a purely platonic way, of course. I mean, Jay seemed like an awesome guy, and messing around with his girlfriend would not be a cool thing to do. Then again, if she tried to seduce me, I'm not sure I'd be able to turn her down.

Oh, yeah, right. I couldn't even talk to Semi-Hot Sandra at the Concierge Lounge without sounding like a complete douchebag. My chances of getting seduced by Snow White were less than zero.

But that didn't mean it wasn't fun to think about....

10

—After we'd finished eating, Jay walked me up a ramp and into the employee parking lot. I spied the limo parked all the way in the far corner. Fuck yeah, traveling in style.

We strode up to the limo like a couple of badasses. If it had been a movie we would've been going in slow-mo. Cast Members stared at us, and I was feeling like a rock star.

Jay opened the back door of the limo, and my cool demeanor immediately flew north for the summer when I saw Lisa in the backseat, a glass of champagne in one hand, and a bottle of some sort of makeup remover in the other. She was wearing a green flannel and jeans, and was, astoundingly, even hotter without her costume and makeup.

"Hey there, handsome," she said in that low, husky, sultry voice. "Why don't you stop staring and get in the fucking car?"

Holy shit. Snow White had a foul mouth!

"Uh, yep, that's, uh, yeah…" I mumbled incoherently, as I slid into the backseat of the limo.

Jay pointed to me. "Lisa, this is Blaine. Blaine, this is Lisa. Give the man a drink, Lisa, and watch your language!"

"Aye aye, Captain!" she said, saluting at him as he rolled his eyes and closed the door.

She shoved a glass in my hand. "What's your poison, dear?"

"Um, I, uh, mostly I drink, um…" Fuck!

"Champagne it is!" she said, pouring me a glass from the already half-empty bottle.

"Thanks," I managed to get out.

"Everything okay back there?" asked Jay, rolling down the divider and turning to us from the front seat.

"Everything is awesome, baby! I'm gonna make Blaine help me with the Dermablend remover, since I know you hate the smell."

"That would be great! You okay with that, Blaine?"

"What's Dermablend?" I asked.

"You'll see," said Jay. "You're going to love this, Blaine. And if you don't mind, I'm going to put the barrier up so I don't have to smell that stuff. It gives me a headache."

"Uh... what?" I asked, worried I'd really gotten myself into some crazy shit here.

The divider rose, and Lisa and I were alone in the backseat of a limo.

"Put your champagne down. You're going to need both hands for this," she said.

I obediently put my glass into the cup-holder and she shoved a paper towel and the bottle of makeup remover into my hand.

"I really only need help with the back of my neck and shoulders," said Lisa. "I can get the rest of it."

She unbuttoned her flannel shirt down to below her breasts. She wasn't wearing a bra, and the shirt was just barely covering her nipples. This was awesome.

"Sorry if I'm coming across as completely ignorant," I said, flustered, "but I honestly don't know what's going on here. Is this like some normal chick thing, or does Disney make you wear some weird special makeup, or is it like..."

"Dude, I'm about to show you my tits," she said, cutting me off.

"Really?" I asked.

"Yeah, really. But only if you'll stop asking questions, put the makeup remover on the paper towel, and wipe my neck!"

I fumbled with the bottle and spilled a bit on my pants.

"Careful! That shit's expensive!" shouted Lisa.

"Don't yell at me. I'm already nervous here."

Lisa sighed, and after a bit more fumbling, I finally got some of the liquid onto the paper towel. She turned and let her shirt fall from her shoulders, exposing her neck and back, but also completely uncovering her breasts. She lifted the hair off her neck with one hand, giving me an awesome side-boob view. Man, they were absolutely perfect. So fucking hot. This was total spank bank material.

"Blaine!" she yelled. "Hurry the fuck up, already!"

"Okay!" I said, tearing my gaze from her tits.

I ran the paper towel across her neck and the tops of her shoulders and nearly shit a brick as her skin completely changed color, from tan to all sorts of bright reds and blues. Tattoos! I wiped more, completely forgetting about her tits (well, not completely) as the tattoos revealed themselves. It was amazing. Once I was done, and before she buttoned herself back up, I got a full view: on her left shoulder was Figment in his astronaut outfit, on her neck were the skull and crossbones from Pirates of the Caribbean, and on her right shoulder were the three hitchhiking ghosts from The Haunted Mansion.

She buttoned up her shirt, took the paper towels and makeup remover from me, and started working on her hands. As the makeup slowly disappeared, I saw that each knuckle had one of the old EPCOT Center pavilion icons painted on it, with the main park logo split between the tops of her two hands.

"Omigodnofuckinway!" I shouted

She smiled and put her hands next to each other, showing me how it all fit together.

"And the pavilions are all in geographic order and divided properly between Future World East and West!" I squealed like a total nerd. I couldn't help myself. It was easily one of the coolest things I'd seen.

"Yeah, they are!" she said. "Nobody ever notices that!"

She leaned over and kissed me on the cheek. I blushed, and popped another woody. She looked down at my crotch and smirked.

"You're a nice guy, Blaine. Odd, and a bit sexually frustrated, but nice."

"Uh, thanks? Wait, what? I'm not sexually frustrated!" I paused and thought of the past two nights in the Jacuzzi with Tracey from the Resort Channel. "Oh, wait, yeah. Yeah, I am. Never mind." I sighed. "Can we change the subject?"

"Sure," she said, picking up her champagne. Her EPCOT Center tattooed fingers wrapped around the stem of the glass. Goddamn that was sexy.

"So I guess nobody at work knows you have those?" I asked.

"A few people. Not my managers, though. They wouldn't have hired me if they knew I had them. It's against 'The Disney Look', which is a real book filled with all sorts of restrictions on Cast Members' appearance, like how long your hair can be, and how many rings you can wear on each hand, and how you should pluck your eyebrows, and just tons of crazy shit like that. Tattoos are right at the top of the 'hell no' list, along with piercings. If a Guest ever saw any of them I'd get fired immediately. So I spend a shitload on this Dermablend crap. But it works really well."

"It doesn't rub off on your costume?"

"No, there's a setting powder that keeps that from happening. It's all very involved and expensive, and it took me a while to get it perfect. But I think it's worth it. The hands are the most difficult, so I considered getting the knuckle tattoos removed. But I really like them, so I figure I'll just keep pulling one over on The Mouse."

"Yeah, the knuckle ones are awesome."

"Thanks. It's fun to show them off to an appreciative audience." She smiled at me, and refilled her glass. "So how do you know Jay?"

"He picked me up at the airport a few days ago. Literally. Like, I was all drunk and he picked me up and I puked on his shoes, and…." This was not a good story to be telling a hot girl.

"And? And, what? And then you had buttsex?"

"What? No, we didn't have buttsex! What the fuck?"

She doubled over laughing. It was a lovely, musical laugh, even if it was at my expense. I wanted to hear that laugh a lot more.

"So what about you two?" I asked, honestly curious. "How did you meet?"

"Well, it's hard not to notice Jay. He'd been coming to the parks daily since way before I started working there, and everybody knew him and knew he was cool. So I wasn't like creeped out or anything when I started noticing him standing around during my princess meet-and-greets. My handler was good friends with him…"

I stopped her. "Your what?"

"My handler? It's the person who stays with the characters at all times while they're onstage. You've never noticed that? All of the characters always have a Cast Member with them to make sure they don't get manhandled, and to make sure they get backstage safely and in a manner that doesn't disturb the Guests' "magic". So the handlers are always like, 'Snow White has to go cook for the dwarfs now!' or some shit like that. As opposed to, 'Snow White is sweating like a fucking pig out here and seriously needs to take a piss!' You get the idea, right?"

"Yeah, yeah. I guess it's just so seamless and coordinated that I never paid attention. Wow."

"Well, good. That's how it's supposed to be. Anyway, my handler knew Jay and invited me to a party at his place, and I guess we just sorta hit it off. Obviously I'm a big fan of Disney tattoos, so I spent the whole night looking at his, and he spent the whole night looking at all of mine," she motioned to her back, "and so one thing led to another, and…. Well, he's such a sweet guy and he really likes taking care of people, and I guess that's kind of what I needed and wanted."

I noticed that "needed" and "wanted" were past tense. I wondered if that was intentional….

"Anyway," she continued, "that's the way it happened! Any other questions, Mr. Paparazzi?"

"I'm sorry, I didn't mean to pry," I said, embarrassed.

"Dude, it was a joke!" She laughed at me again. "You can pry all you want. Just know that maybe sometimes you won't like some of the answers, okay?"

"Okay. I probably just need to shut up, honestly."

"No, no, it's good, everything is cool. I'm enjoying my conversation with you, Blaine. Honestly."

She put her hand on my leg. And, predictably, my erection returned in full-force.

"And you obviously like talking to me!" she said.

"Jesus, I need to wear baggier pants or something. This is ridiculously embarrassing."

"Don't worry about it. It's sorta my job, right? Like, making people feel happy and excited and shit? I mean, there's a reason why Walt didn't make the princes and princesses butt-ugly. He knew the dads and moms were the ones spending the cash on the movies and merchandise. The man wasn't dumb. Make Snow White a hottie and the dads aren't gonna mind so much sitting through the movie, buying the dolls, and shelling out the cash so their kids could meet her in real life. It's definitely a fine line appealing to both the kids and the adults." She flipped her hair, batted her eyes, and spoke in what was her imitation of Snow White's voice, "But I think I pull it off pretty well, don't you?"

"Yes. Yes, you do," I lied. The voice was terrible. But she was so beautiful and nice that I couldn't imagine anyone complaining, and I certainly wasn't going to be the first.

She smiled, obviously pleased with her performance, and my subsequent praise.

"So, what about you, Blaine? What's your story? Retired porn star, maybe? You certainly don't have any trouble getting it up!"

"What? No! Leave my penis alone!" I yelled.

The divider rolled down.

"Did I just hear what I think I heard?" asked Jay. He looked down. "Oh, good. Everybody's pants are still on. Don't mind me."

The divider rolled back up, and Lisa burst out laughing.

"You made him jealous!" she said.

"What? No, no, no!"

I banged on the partition.

"Jay, nothing is happening back here, I swear!"

The partition cracked a bit, and Jay's voice filtered through it.

"Drink more champagne, Blaine. You're way too uptight"

The divider closed again, and Lisa had a giggling fit that was so damned cute that I… well, I didn't do anything. I just sat there with a stupid grin on my face, totally falling for this girl.

She stopped laughing, and wiped a tear from her eye. "Oh, shit. I haven't laughed like that in a while."

"Glad I could be of service. Now, can we please leave my junk out of any future discussions?"

"I'm sorry, Blaine. I didn't mean to… it's just that you're like a little middle school kid! You're like someone I'd babysit!"

"What the fuck? No, I'm not! First of all, I'm thirty years old. And secondly, how many middle school kids do you know who are multi-millionaires?"

Well, that shut her up.

"You're a multi-millionaire?" she asked, quietly, and with a sort of growl that made my downstairs bits all tingly again.

"Yeah, that's what I was about to explain before you started going on about me being a porn star and shit. Yes, I have multiple millions of dollars in my bank accounts. I'm crazy stupid rich and it's not as awesome as you think it is."

She looked at me, obviously a bit stunned.

"Look," I said, "it really isn't all that it's cracked up to be. I'm a grown ass man living at Walt Disney World. That should tell you something about the price I paid for my elite millionaire status," I said, stressing the "elite" sarcastically.

Lisa was silent. Just staring at me. It was weird, but I didn't mind her being captivated by me for a change.

"You're going to get along really well with our dinner guests tonight, Blaine. I think they're…" she paused, "I think we're your kind of people."

"I don't know what my kind of people are," I said.

"I'm your kind of people," she said, moving closer.

I downed my champagne, reached over her, grabbed the bottle, poured another glass, downed that, and laughed.

"Well, if they're all like you, then yeah, it's going to be one helluva night!"

11

—The limo pulled up to Jay's house, and I started to open the door. Lisa smacked my hand out of the way.

"Don't open the door!" she said. "Let Jay do it."

"I'm fully capable of opening a door, Lisa," I said, pulling at the handle again.

She hit me harder.

"Ah, bitch, what the fuck?" I yelled.

"Let the man do his job, Blaine."

"He's not on the clock. I'm not paying him anymore."

"Let the man do his job," she said sternly. "This limo is one of the few things he has total control over. Don't take that away from him."

"Fine, whatever. Fucking weirdo."

Jay opened the door and Lisa stepped out. I followed.

"I could've opened…" I started to say.

"Welcome back to Jay's Castle!" said Lisa, interrupting.

Jay swept his hands in a grand gesture. "Jay's Castle, indeed! And maybe this time, Mr. McKinnon, it'll be Jay's Castle with 99% less vomit?"

"Haha, very funny," I said. Except that I was already a bit drunk. I guess I did need to watch myself this evening. Puking all over my shirt again would be pretty lame.

"The other guests should be arriving shortly," he said as he unlocked the door and we stepped inside, "so I need to start cooking! Please make yourself at home. You know where the facilities are." He winked at me.

Shit, he totally knew I rooted through his stuff the other day. Oh well. If he didn't care then neither did I.

"Feel free to partake in my vast film collection while you wait," he said. "I have a lot of rare promotional Disney films on 16mm. Lisa can show you how to play them."

He walked off into the kitchen, once again leaving me and Lisa alone.

She swallowed her champagne.

"I need another drink. How about you?" she asked.

"Gin and tonic, please?"

"Sure. You want to see something really awesome?" she asked.

"The promo films sounded pretty cool," I replied.

She walked over to Jay's bar, a black wooden cart sort of thing, on wheels.

"This is a portable bar that was used at private parties in The Magic Kingdom." She poured out a shot of gin. "They'd wheel it out for companies who would rent sections of the park after-hours. Normally there's no booze allowed in The Magic Kingdom, but Event Services makes an exception if you have enough cash."

She finished putzing around behind the bar and handed me the gin and tonic. It had a glow cube in it, just like the at the resort bars.

"And you, Mr. Millionaire," she said, "definitely have enough cash."

"Yes, I suppose I do," I replied, not knowing how to react, and slightly turned off. Was she a money-grubber or something? Was that why she was attracted to Jay? Because he had money? Did he have money? I guess he must be loaded to be able to buy all this memorabilia. Man, that would suck if she just used guys for their money. I'd already had my fill of that shit with Connie.

She turned away, obviously sensing my discomfort.

"Anyway, that's not the cool thing. Check this shit out."

She flipped a switch on the wall and neon lit up everywhere

around the bar, including a kick ass Pleasure Island sign. There were also blinking "movie" lights around a Mickey-shaped mirror on the wall, flanked by two lava lamps held by white-gloved Mouse hands.

"Nice!" I said, sitting down on the couch, admiring the light show.

She sat next to me, placing her martini on the mirror table.

"So c'mon, tell me! What do, or what did, you do for a living, Blaine?" she asked.

Something about the martini reminded me of a party in a movie where someone was asked a similar question....

"Just one word: Plastics," I responded, mimicking my favorite bit from *The Graduate.*

She didn't get it.

"Plastics?"

"There's a great future in plastics," I continued.

"I don't really like plastic," she said.

That cracked me up.

"Why are you laughing at me?" she said angrily, obviously not used to anyone pulling one over on her.

"No, no, I'm kidding. It's from *The Graduate!*"

She looked at me blankly.

"You know, *The Graduate* with Dustin Hoffman? Simon & Garfunkel songs? Anne Bancroft seduces him? No? Really? You've never seen *The Graduate?*"

"No, I haven't," she said.

"Well, shit! That was Walt Disney's favorite movie," I said.

"Really?" she said.

"Yeah, really. Apparently he watched it over and over. Diane Disney Miller said she always suspected her dad had a big crush on Anne Bancroft. He tried to cast her in several films but she kept turning him down because she thought he was a pervert."

"No fucking way!"

"Yeah.... No. I'm totally making this shit up. But you should still watch the movie. It's awesome."

Lisa hit me with a Mickey pillow. Hard. And then she hit me again, harder.

"You motherfucker!" she yelled, but smiling now.

"Bitch, stop hitting me!"

Jay popped his head out of the kitchen.

"Now, children. Please behave!"

"He's lying to me, Jay!" shouted Lisa.

"The woman has never seen *The Graduate!*" I shouted back.

"She's from a different generation, Blaine. These kids have no appreciation for anything that wasn't popular fifteen minutes ago."

"Hey!" said Lisa.

"How the fuck old are you, anyway?" I asked.

"Twenty-three," she said.

"Holy shit, Jay, you're a goddamned cradle-robber!"

Jay chuckled. "And proud of it," he said as he sauntered back into the kitchen.

"Twenty-three?" I said, turning to Lisa. "Twenty-three!"

"So what, asshole?" she responded.

"Man, when I was twenty-three…. Actually, nothing good happened when I was twenty-three. Nothing good really happened between seventeen and now…." I paused. I was definitely tipsy. "But this is good. I like this."

"Yeah, this is nice. You're fun to be around."

"Ah, well, thank you very much! If you have any hot friends or relatives who you think might be interested in a rich, vaguely handsome albeit socially awkward dude, please send them all my way!"

"No chance," said Lisa. "I'm keeping you all to myself."

"Plastics," I said, snickering.

"Fucker," she said. "Seriously, tell me what you used to do for a living."

"Oh, it's so boring. I started a computer repair company out in Baltimore. Like Geek Squad except for small-to-medium sized businesses. Got a bunch of clients, made a bunch of money, sold the business, made even more money. The end."

"You're right. Boring!"

"Told you so. That was my life from high school until now. Lived and breathed the business."

"So what brought you to Florida?"

"I had nothing left in Baltimore. And some shit went down, and I didn't want to be there anymore. And I remembered being happy at Walt Disney World, so I came here. I'm just trying to have a good time, and maybe deal with some things. But mostly I want to have fun. I haven't had fun since I was a kid."

The doorbell rang.

"Well, tonight should be a blast!" she said, getting up and walking to the door. "Just do me a favor, and try to get past your first impressions of these people. I know they're a bit... odd on the surface. But they're all really nice once you get to know them."

"Uh, okay?"

She opened the door, and greeted a couple.

"Belinda! Michael! How nice to see you! Oh, and you've brought the baby!"

"Hi, Lisa," said Michael.

"Very nice to see you again, Lisa," said Belinda.

"Jay is in the kitchen cooking up his usual recipes, but here, let me introduce you to someone new to our group."

Lisa walked the couple over to me. They looked like regular thirty-something suburban parents. Except that the woman was cradling a white towel with a blue knit beanie laid on top of it.

What. The. Fuck.

"Belinda and Michael, this is Blaine McKinnon. He's here all the way from Baltimore!"

"Hi," I said, shaking Michael's hand.

"This is our son," said Belinda.

"Oh." I looked at Lisa, who was behind them.

She mouthed "Say 'hello' to the baby!"

"Hello, baby," I said. "You're very cute."

"How sweet," said Belinda. "Thank you."

"Would you two like a drink?" asked Lisa.

"Sure," said Belinda. "How about one of your famous glow-tinis? And maybe some apple juice for the baby?"

"Coming right up!" said Lisa, ducking behind the bar.

"Get me one, too," I yelled.

"Sssh, not so loud," said Belinda. "You'll wake him."

"Oh, shit. Sorry about that."

Belinda scowled and turned away from me. Michael shrugged.

"Lisa, dearest," said Belinda, "do you mind if we pop into the kitchen to give our greetings to the host?"

"Sure, no problem, I'm sure he'd love an extra hand in there."

As soon as they walked into the kitchen I ran over to Lisa. I put my hands up and stared at her with my best "WTF" face.

"What?" she asked, pouring various types of booze into a cocktail shaker.

"What do you mean, 'what'?" I said. "The baby! What the fuck is with the baby?"

"It's a towel, Blaine."

"No shit, it's a towel, Lisa. Why do they think it's a baby?"

"I think they know it's a towel. Or, at least, Michael knows." She shook the cocktail shaker violently, unscrewed the cap, and poured out the blue liquid into three martini glasses. "Last year Belinda had a baby who died a few days after he was born. She hasn't been able to get over it. The baby died on that towel in the hospital."

"Damn, that's terrible. So, they just walk around with it everywhere?"

"Yeah, they're at the parks every day, walking around with the towel baby. Is that a problem? Are you going to be an asshole about this?"

"No, but, it's just bizarre."

"You're a thirty year old man living at Disney World, Blaine."

"Yeah, but…"

"But nothing. You told me you were here to have fun and get over some shit. They're no different than you."

She popped a glow cube into each martini glass, handed me

mine, and walked into the kitchen with the other two, leaving me alone in the living room.

"Am I as messed up as those people?" I thought. It didn't sit well, but I couldn't deny Lisa's logic. Before I had time to think about it anymore the doorbell rang again.

"Blaine, can you get that please?" yelled Jay from the kitchen.

"Sure," I yelled back.

I opened the door and standing in front of me was what appeared to be Princess Leia, straight out of *A New Hope*. Except her classic side-of-the-head buns were wound with bright red hair, not brown like the real Leia. And her outfit! Her white gown was made from thin, transparent gauze. I could see right through it. The carpet seemed to match the drapes.

"Hi!" she said. She was very perky. "I'm Theresa Skywalker! Is Jay here?"

"Yeah," I said. I could see her tits pretty clearly. "He's in the kitchen."

"Who are you?"

"Oh, sorry. I'm Blaine McKinnon. I'm living at The Beach Club."

"Living there?"

"Yeah."

"Cool!"

"Thanks. Uh. Sorry, come in," I said, realizing she was still standing outside. Her nipples were clearly getting harder from the evening breeze.

She wasn't horrible looking, by any stretch.

"I think I feel Miss Nancy's presence behind me," said Theresa Skywalker.

"Miss Nancy?"

Theresa Skywalker looked out the door. "Yep, there she is! Her husband died last year. But The Force is strong in her."

"I bet."

"Hi, Miss Nancy!" said Theresa Skywalker. "Can we help you with your suitcases?"

"That would be lovely, Terry," said Miss Nancy, who seemed normal enough. She looked like a grandmother from a 50s sitcom. Kinda dowdy, with a sweater, scarf, and long patterned dress covering her ample figure.

"Actually, can you get them, Blaine?" asked Theresa Skywalker. "My Force lifting abilities have been in a weakened state since my lightsaber fight with Lord Vader earlier today."

"That's a shame." I picked up the two suitcases and brought them into the house.

"Right by the sofa, dear," said Miss Nancy. "Your name is Blaine?"

"Yes, ma'am," I said.

She opened her suitcases, started pulling out stuffed bears, and began to arrange them on the sofa.

"Very nice to meet you, Blaine. I'm Miss Nancy."

"Hello, Miss Nancy."

She pulled the last of the teddy bears from the second suitcase, precariously balanced it next to another one on the loveseat, and patted it on the head. "Perfect," she said.

Jay poked his head out of the kitchen. "Terry! Miss Nancy! Come on in! Dinner is almost ready!" He looked over at me. "Blaine, I hate to do this, but can you set the table? All of the plates and silverware are right there in the cabinet in the dining room."

"Sure, Jay, no problem."

Miss Nancy and Theresa Skywalker went into the kitchen with everyone else.

"Man, where's a fucking camera when you need one?" I thought.

I set the table with Jay's nice Grand Floridian gold-rimmed plates. All of his silverware had plastic handles shaped like various vintage Disney characters.

After I finished setting the table I stood around for a minute like a dumbass, waiting for everyone to come out. It was really quiet in the kitchen. Too quiet, considering the number of people in there.

I pushed open the door very slightly and saw everyone standing around Miss Nancy as she snorted a huge line of sparkling white powder off the kitchen counter. Then Belinda snorted a line. She pushed the towel across some of it, too.

It was all sorts of fucked up.

I continued watching as Theresa Skywalker sniffed a line. And then, much to my dismay, so did Lisa.

That sucked.

Jay gestured to Michael, who shook his head "no". Well, at least he wasn't a total fucking junkie.

Shit. Fuck these people. I was outta there.

I started walking to the door and remembered I didn't have a car. Jay had driven me there. Fuck. I'd have to call a cab. But I couldn't do it there and cause a huge scene. I figured it'd be better if I just left and started walking. I seemed to remember there being a gas station a few blocks down. I'd meet the cab there.

I opened the door and stepped out into the surprisingly chilly evening air. I wished I'd brought a jacket, but it'd been in the mid-80s that morning. Oh well. I walked quickly, hands in my jean pockets, already shivering. I only got to the end of the block before I heard Lisa yelling my name.

"What the fuck, Blaine?" she said, breathlessly running up to me.

"It's okay. I'm fine. I'm just going to head on home, and didn't want to interrupt the party. Thanks for having me over."

I turned and headed towards the main road.

"Fuck you, Blaine!" shouted Lisa.

"Real nice," I muttered.

She ran up to me. I increased my pace. She matched my speed.

"So, what? You saw us in the kitchen, I guess? And that's it, you're leaving, just like that? Who the fuck do you think you are?"

"I'm not a goddamned junkie, that's for sure!" I shouted.

"You have no idea what was going on in there."

"I know what I saw."

"It wasn't what it looked like. Anyway, who are you to judge?

You're going to puke and piss all over my boyfriend's limo and then judge me for doing something that makes me feel happy? At least I'm still conscious and not destroying someone's property!"

She had a point. But, still…. I stopped walking.

"That's harsh," I said. "Yeah, maybe I was drinking so I didn't have to deal with some stuff. But believe me, I'm trying to deal with it. And just because we've both done dumb shit doesn't make either one of us right. It just means we're both idiots."

"Whatever. Everyone in there has problems, Blaine, and we're all just trying to keep it together day-by-day, okay? I figured maybe you could relate to that… I guess I was wrong."

I sighed. "No, look, you're not wrong. I can relate. I just… it was a bit much, okay? I mean, between the teddy bears and the see-through Princess Leia outfit, and the fucking towel baby…. The drugs pushed me over the edge."

She stepped back, relaxing her posture a bit.

"Man, this stuff is starting to kick in and you're totally killing my buzz," she said. "Can we please go back inside?"

"I don't know, Lisa." We stared at each other.

Goddamn she was gorgeous.

"Maybe this'll convince you?" she said, pulling me closer.

She kissed me, and it was incredible, but all I could think was, "Holy shit! Snow White is actually seducing me!" Like, I couldn't truly enjoy the awesomeness of what was happening because it was just so fucking unbelievable.

But then an image of Jay's tattoos, all the Disney characters screaming "No!", blasted into my mind, and I pulled away quickly.

"What's wrong?" she asked.

"It's Jay," I said. "I can't…"

She kissed me again before I could finish the sentence. I didn't resist. Something about her taste and smell was so intoxicating…. I didn't stand a chance. I'd probably do whatever this girl wanted.

After what was easily the longest, most mind-blowing kiss I'd ever experienced, she pulled away.

"Holy shit," I said. I was shaking.

"I've been planning on leaving him anyway," she said, matter-of-factly. "Maybe you were just the kick in the pants I needed."

I was still in la-la land, and it took me a second to comprehend what she was saying.

"Wait, what?!" I shouted, finally. "No way!"

"What do you mean, 'no way'?" she asked. "Don't you like me?"

"Oh, hell yeah. Yeah, you have no idea. But Jay.... Nobody deserves to be cheated on, especially not someone as nice as him. It totally wouldn't be cool for me to steal his girlfriend."

I couldn't believe I was actually turning this girl down. Was I a total fucking idiot?

"I'm leaving him either way, Blaine. It's just a matter of when."

"That's great," I said, "and I hope you'll call me the second you're gone. I'll be like the fucking Road Runner. I'll be at your door before you even hang up the phone. But I can't be the reason why you leave. I can't have more bad shit on my conscience. Does that make sense?"

She smiled. "I can't say I'm not disappointed, but I understand. You're a good guy."

"Christ, you want to talk about being disappointed?" I said, putting my hands on her hips. "Not being able to do this again is going to suck."

I kissed her, and tried my hardest to remember everything about it. Because I had no idea if something this awesome was going to happen to me again anytime soon.

I stepped back and she had a great dreamy look on her face.

"Goddamn," she said slowly.

"I know, right?" I said. I took her arm. "Let's go back inside, okay?"

"Yeah, definitely," she said, pushing close to me. "It's fucking freezing out here!"

"Theresa Skywalker's nipples certainly seemed to think so," I said.

"I saw! That bitch has some tits, huh?"

"Maybe I can use some Jedi Mind Tricks to get her to let me

touch 'em?"

Lisa smacked me. "Pig!"

We both laughed and walked back to the house.

I fully expected to get grilled when we returned, but Jay never asked where we'd been. If he had any suspicions about us, he didn't let on. And I certainly never brought it up. I felt weird about it, but shit, how many other guys would've stopped an ultra-hot Snow White from seducing them? Not many, that's for fucking sure. I might not have handled the situation perfectly or anything, but at least I was still a decent friend.

12

—Some of my favorite snippets from the party that night:

AT THE DINNER TABLE

> THERESA SKYWALKER
> Luke has fallen to the dark side. I don't think I want to be married to him anymore.

> LISA
> But didn't you just have your last name legally changed to "Skywalker"?

> THERESA SKYWALKER
> Yeah, but if he's going to keep denying me access to his, uh, lightsaber, then I don't know how this marriage can continue! Plus, I think I have a crush on Ron Stoppable.

> MISS NANCY
> Ooh, you mean the one who walks around with Kim Possible at The Studios? He's so sexy.

> LISA
> Miss Nancy!

MISS NANCY

What? Just because I'm old doesn't mean I don't find men attractive. For example, young Blaine here is quite a treat.

ME

Uh, thanks, Miss Nancy. You're… uh… not so bad yourself?

EVERYONE

(laughter)

ALONE IN THE KITCHEN WITH MICHAEL

MICHAEL

You know it's just a towel, right?

ME

Yeah.

MICHAEL

Oh, good. Sometimes I get a little confused. When everyone else is talking to a towel like it's a baby, you start to wonder whether you're the crazy one.

SITTING ON THE COUCH ACROSS FROM MISS NANCY, ENVELOPED BY HER TEDDY BEARS

ME

So if you don't mind me asking, why teddy bears?

MISS NANCY

Oh, I don't mind, dear. My husband had a very

sweet tradition of buying me a teddy bear on our anniversary each year. We were married forty-one years. I saved all of them, and they're in fairly good shape, all things considered.

ME

That's pretty amazing. Such a cool idea, too. I'm totally going to steal it if I ever get married.

MISS NANCY

Yes, he was a very kind man, and I miss him very much....

ALONE IN THE KITCHEN WITH BELINDA

ME

Your baby is very cute.

BELINDA

It's a towel!

ME

Right... a baby towel.

BELINDA

No, just a towel! What are you, some kind of idiot?

RUNNING INTO THERESA SKYWALKER AS I EXITED THE BATHROOM

ME

Hi!

THERESA SKYWALKER
Do you like my dress?

ME
Yes, it's quite… revealing.

THERESA SKYWALKER
Would you like to cum all over my tits?

ME
Jesus. Uh. Maybe later?

THERESA SKYWALKER
Luke has a huge lightsaber.

ME
Good to know. Bye!

ALONE IN THE KITCHEN WITH MICHAEL

ME
So she knows it's a towel?

MICHAEL
She does?

ME
Seriously?

MICHAEL
I never bring it up.

ME
I told her the baby was cute and she told me it
was a towel and that I was an idiot.

MICHAEL

Huh. Interesting.

ME

So if you both know it's just a towel, then why is she still carrying it around?

MICHAEL

Beats me. It's better than her crying all day.

ME

Oh. Yeah, that's true.

AT THE DINNER TABLE

JAY

You're just propagating the lies, Blaine!

ME

What?

LISA

Yeah, what's next, Blaine? You gonna start saying he hated Jews?

ME

Of course not!

JAY

The point is, the fact that an intelligent person like you is buying into those same old urban legends is disturbing.

ME

I was just asking a question! Is the man's head in cryo-freeze or not?

LISA

Cryo-freeze? This isn't *Star Trek*, Blaine!

MICHAEL

What the hell is cryo-freeze?

ME

I don't know. It was a simple question. I'm just asking because I thought someone here might know.

JAY

He was cremated. I actually have some of his ashes.

EVERYONE

What?!

MISS NANCY

My husband was put into cryo-freeze.

EVERYONE

What?!

AT THE BAR WITH LISA

ME

Theresa Skywalker wants me to cum all over her tits.

LISA

Are you going to?

ME

I don't know. I don't want her stalking me.

LISA

She probably would stalk you.

ME

She does have nice tits, though.

LISA

Let me put it this, way, Blaine. If you fuck
Theresa Skywalker you will never fuck me.

ME

Oh.

LISA

And you have a pretty good chance of fucking
me.

ME

Oh!

LISA

So don't cum on Theresa Skywalker's tits.

ME

Okay.

AT THE DINNER TABLE

ME

So nobody cares that you sit in the lobby at The
Grand Floridian all day with teddy bears all
around you?

JAY

Miss Nancy doesn't hurt anybody, Blaine. And
the children seem to like the teddy bears.

ME

But the staff is cool with you being there?

MISS NANCY

If you had any idea how much my husband and
I spent at The Grand Floridian over the years,
you wouldn't be asking that question. We used
to stay for months at a time, and we were always
very generous to the staff.

ME

Wow.

MISS NANCY

My husband also bequeathed a healthy sum to
help The Disney Family start development on a
museum celebrating Walt's life. I think it would
be quite improper for them to not allow me to
enjoy the grounds of their hotel.

LISA

Miss Nancy, you better tell me if anyone ever
gives you any trouble. I swear I'll cut a bitch!

MISS NANCY

I'm sure that won't be necessary dear. If anybody bothers me I'll simply have them fired.

ME

Damn. That's hardcore.

MISS NANCY

Indeed.

ALONE IN THE KITCHEN WITH MICHAEL

ME

So, maybe this is a strange thing to bring up, but why weren't you doing drugs with everyone else?

MICHAEL

You saw that?

ME

Yeah. I saw you turn them down.

MICHAEL

Man, you weren't supposed to see any of that.

ME

But I did.

MICHAEL

Shit. Look, it's simple, Blaine. I don't want to miss out on anything life has to offer. When our baby died, it was the worst thing that ever happened to me. I've tried this drug, and it really does make everything seem… magical. But I didn't want my baby dying to seem magical. That's just a bastardization of reality, and it demeans the life of my son, as brief as it was.

ME

I think I can relate to that.

MICHAEL

Well, you've obviously been through some shit, then. And that's not a bad thing. I don't think that someone can truly appreciate real happiness without experiencing real tragedy. You need contrast in life. If all you see are the beautiful things… well, you become numb to them.

ME

So why do you let her do it?

MICHAEL

Because all she saw was the tragedy. She stopped being able to see the beautiful things. They all did.

13

—The party broke up relatively early, as Theresa Skywalker absolutely had to get to MGM Studios by eleven AM the next day to see Ron Stoppable's first performance. Michael and Belinda had to, no shit, "take care of the baby." And Miss Nancy, bless her old heart, was starting to nod off on the loveseat.

I stayed at Jay's, crashing on the couch. Lisa stayed the night, too, which sucked. Knowing she was in his bedroom, probably fucking him, made me extraordinarily jealous. Luckily I hadn't gotten too drunk, so I didn't do or say anything inappropriate around him that would make him think something was going on between me and Lisa. But the downside of not being drunk was that I stayed awake all night picturing the two of them in the bedroom together. Ugh.

The next morning, after maybe two hours of sleep, I woke up to the sound of Lisa yelling.

"What the fuck, Jay? You're going to start charging me for The Dust now? I'm your fucking girlfriend!"

Indecipherable mumbling from Jay.

"I don't give a damn about profit margins or costs or any of that shit," yelled Lisa. "How about I start charging you to fuck me? And you'd better bet the costumes and role-playing will be extra, you fucking pervert!"

More quiet, seemingly calm talking from Jay that I couldn't make out.

"What? No, of course you can't borrow money from me! I'm living paycheck to paycheck as it is. Sell some of your Disney shit!"

Slightly louder response from Jay. I could make out, "…need the money now," but that was about it.

"Well, that was pretty poor planning on your part, but there's no way you're dragging me down with you."

Jay's voice was low again. Really low.

"Are you threatening me? I'm getting off that shit anyway! I don't need it anymore. Fuck this. I'm outta here."

A door slammed, and Lisa came running out into the living room, phone in hand.

"I need a cab at 9615 Gamling Lane. As fast as you can, please."

"Shit, Lisa. Really?" I said, sitting up and rubbing the crust from my eyes.

"I told you, Blaine. That was the last straw. Bastard is trying to charge me for The Dust? Total bullshit. I don't need him or The Dust."

"Yeah, sure," I said, stunned. It was all very surreal.

Jay came storming out of the room, naked. Lovely.

"Lisa, I forbid you to leave!" he said, his voice fairly calm.

"You may own all this Disney shit," said Lisa, gesturing around the house. "But you don't own this princess."

She walked out the door and he followed, apparently too wound up to bother putting clothes on.

Great. Now there was a fat naked man with a body full of tattoos chasing a hot chick down the road. This certainly wouldn't draw any attention. I watched them, Lisa screaming obscenities at him, while he just stood there and took it, occasionally interjecting to no avail.

But then she must have said something really nasty, because he grabbed her shoulders and started shaking her.

"You're hurting me!" I heard her yell.

I barely remember grabbing the empty champagne bottle and running out to them.

"Jay," I said slowly, the bottle raised in a striking position next to his head. "I'm only half awake right now, but I will absolutely break this bottle over your head. Please take your hands off Lisa and go back into the house." I glanced at his shrunken cock. "And for Christ's sake, put some goddamned clothes on."

He immediately let go of her.

"Blaine...." He looked down at his naked body. "I...." He looked at Lisa, who was crying.

"I'm so sorry," he said, and ran back into the house.

Lisa and I stood there staring at each other. I didn't know what to say. It was strange seeing someone so strong-willed looking so weak and vulnerable. I wanted to comfort her, to wipe her tears away, to do something to make her feel better. But shit, if Jay was watching, who knew what he'd do in the state he was in?

The cab pulled up and Lisa got in.

"I'll call you in a few days," she said.

"Promise?"

"Yeah."

The cab drove off, and I was surprised to find myself choking up. It was something about the tone of her voice. I was pretty sure she wasn't going to be calling me. And that sucked, because I was in love with her. I mean, I'd certainly never threatened to break a champagne bottle over anyone's head for a chick before.... That must be love, right?

I didn't have much time to dwell on it, because right then a cop car pulled up.

"Shit," I said.

The officer, a burly guy, got out of the car.

"Hello, Officer," I said weakly.

"Sir, we've received a report of a possible domestic violence situation," he said.

"Yeah...." I said. "Everything's okay now. Everyone's fine. She just drove off in a cab, and he's back in the house now. Nobody got hurt."

"May I ask why you're holding that bottle in your hand?" he asked.

"Oh. Right. Um, it looked like maybe things were getting a little out of hand. So I came out here to break it up."

"That's the job of the police, sir. If you'd hit someone with that bottle you could have been charged with aggravated assault."

"Really?"

"Absolutely. And the male suspect is back in the house?"

"Yeah, Jay."

"Do you think I could talk to him?"

"Sure. I mean, I guess. Hopefully he's put some clothes on."

"So the suspect was nude in public?"

"Shit. Yeah."

We walked up to the house and the officer knocked on the door. Jay opened it, wearing a sweat suit. He seemed totally chilled.

"Hello, Officer," he said.

"I was called here on a possible domestic violence incident. Do you mind if I ask you a few questions?"

"Sure, no problem."

"Can I come inside?" asked the officer.

"It's a bit of a mess," said Jay. "Can we talk out here?"

The officer paused. I saw something cross his face. Suspicion?

"Of course," he said, after a second. "Full name?"

"Jason Montgomery."

"Mr. Montgomery, is it true that you were out on that corner, arguing with a female, while in a state of undress?"

"Yes, sir."

"Okay," said the officer. "I'm going to have to bring you in for public indecency. You have the right to remain silent. Anything you say or do can and will be held against you in a court of law. You have the right to talk to a lawyer before answering any of our questions. If you cannot afford to hire a lawyer, one will be appointed for you without cost and before any questioning. You have the right to use any of these rights at any time you want during this interview. Do you understand these rights as they have been read to you?"

"I do," said Jay.

"And if the female in question decides to press charges, that will also be an aggravated assault charge. At the very least it sounds like she definitely has grounds for a restraining order. Please turn around so I can place the handcuffs on you."

"Yes, sir, Officer," said Jay, without any sign of emotion.

"Jesus," I said.

"Thank you for your help, sir" the officer said as he led Jay towards the police car. "And in the future, please don't even think about hitting someone with a bottle."

Jay turned to me. "I'm sorry about this, Blaine. The keys to the limo are on the nightstand in my bedroom, if you want to drive yourself back. Please don't bail me out."

"What?"

He yelled back as the door closed. "Do not bail me out!"

I stood there as the police car drove off. He was obviously not in his right mind.

About five hours later, once his bail had been set at $3K, and once I'd figured out how to drive that damned limo, I was at the police station, bailing him out.

"I told you not to bail me out," he said.

"You're welcome," I responded. "Can you please drive me back to The Beach Club?"

We drove the whole way there in silence. When we stopped at the entrance I opened the door myself, and got out.

"Let me know if you need anything, okay?" I said.

"I could use some cash," he replied. "I'll probably lose my job at the limo company after all of this. I missed a whole day's worth of pickups, and I imagine they'll find out about the arrest."

"Yeah, man, sure. No problem. How much?"

"Two hundred?"

I pulled three hundred from my wallet and handed it to him.

"This is all I've got on me. Please get your shit together, dude," I said.

"I'm trying, Blaine. I really am."

He hugged me, and all I could think about was how this was

my fault. If I hadn't kissed Lisa, maybe she wouldn't have left, and maybe he wouldn't have gone to jail.

"Call me if you need anything," I said, and walked into the hotel, totally drained. When I got to my room I fell on the bed and passed the fuck out.

14

—The phone woke me up.

"Hello?" I said.

"Mr. McKinnon? It's Charles. I'm at the Belle Vue. Will you be joining me?"

"Oh, shit. Yeah. Sorry, Charles. Rough night. Rough day, actually. You mind waiting about thirty minutes while I get my shit together?"

"No problem. I'm here every Thursday anyway!"

"Okay, cool. See you in a bit."

I couldn't think of a goddamned thing Charles could tell me about Jay that would match what had happened that morning.

Boy was I wrong.

Walking into the Belle Vue Lounge, I was surprised by how low-key it was. A whitewashed wood bar with a polished granite top, surrounded by shelves filled with old games, books, and trinkets. There were plenty of private nooks and crannies, giving the place a bright but intimate olde-tyme feel. It suited Charles perfectly.

I saw him at the bar, drinking what looked to be Scotch, and the best thing was that he was still wearing his Greeter outfit, even though we were the only ones there aside from the bartender.

I pointed to the outfit, smirking.

"Have to keep up appearances while on stage!" he said cheerfully.

"You're a dedicated man, Charles."

"You got that right, Mr. McKinnon. This job is the love of my life."

"Seems like you're very good at it," I said, leaning against the bar. "Speaking of which, I think you can drop the Mr. McKinnon crap when you're not on duty. Just call me Blaine, okay?"

"Sounds fair to me, Blaine!" he said, beaming. "So what'll you have, sire? I'm buying, and don't even try to tell me differently."

"I could desperately use a gin and tonic."

The bartender nodded and poured one of the better gin and tonics I'd ever had. Half a Key lime, some sort of gourmet tonic water, Plymouth gin, and crushed ice. Definitely put me in a better mood.

"Let's sit over here," said Charles, motioning to two chairs and a table overlooking the balcony. "Gorgeous view at sunset."

"Yeah, it's nice," I said. "Look, Charles, I think I pretty much know everything I need to about Jay Montgomery."

"Oh?" said Charles. "And what do you think you know about our friend Jay?"

"I found some article from the Sentinel on Google. He got an inheritance when his dad died, his mom is in a nursing home, he collects Disney shit, he drives a limo… and he's obviously dealing drugs."

Charles nodded, smiling. "You're right about the drugs, son, but the rest is just the same old yarns he's been spinning for years. He's trying to build up some mythology about himself because the reality would be much less appealing to his so-called fans."

"Okay, I'm listening," I said, dubious. Before this morning I probably wouldn't have believed a damned thing Charles had to tell me, but now… I was a little more receptive.

"First of all, his father isn't dead. He lives down in Tarpon Springs and takes care of his mother, who has Alzheimer's."

"But that doesn't make any sense. Then what about the inheritance? How'd he afford to buy all that stuff?"

"I'm getting to that. Anyway, he tells people his father is dead, but really his father disowned him when he left his first wife and their two kids."

"Oh yeah! I saw them in his scrapbook!"

"The way Jay told it to me, he was twenty-two, had a wife who nagged him all the time, but two kids who he really loved. His father was setting him up as the heir to the family business. But Jay wanted nothing to do with the business, or the marriage. He felt like he'd settled down too young and needed to be free. Well, that didn't go over too well with his father, and they got into a big fight. When Jay finally left his wife and kids, his father disowned him. That's when he got his first tattoo, that Snow White one on his shoulder.

"Once he'd left his family, he went hitchhiking around the East Coast, dealing hash for a living. After a few weeks, he figured out that he hadn't budgeted his money very well, and was low on hash. Knowing it was a dangerous business he was in, he'd brought a gun for self-defense. So his bright idea was to use the gun to stick up a convenience store. Now, mind you, he just wanted cash, he didn't want to hurt anyone.

"As he tells it, he was wearing a leather jacket a little too small for him, and the gun is in the pocket, and when he goes to pull out the gun at this cashier, he fumbles it and ends up looking like a buffoon. Eventually he gets the gun out and points it at the cashier, who by his account was a very attractive female.

"'Give me all your money,' he says, realizing how ridiculous it sounds the second it comes out of his mouth.

"Well, this attractive lady takes one look at him and says, 'No.'

"He presses the gun into her, but she still says 'No'.

"You see, she knows he's not going to shoot her in cold blood! She can see it in his eyes that he's no murderer!

"Well, he figures this out pretty quickly, and decides to just run off. He gets maybe a half mile down the road before the county police pick him up and cart him off to jail. He admits everything, pleads guilty to all the charges without even trying to get a plea bargain, and gets sent to the State Penitentiary in New York for ten years.

"He told me he loved it in there. Didn't want to leave. Loved the scheduled activities, loved having someone cook for him, loved having other people manage every second of his life. He didn't have a care in the world in prison. Everyone did everything for him, and all he had to do was pass the time reading, or walking around the grounds, or talking to the other inmates. He told me it was the best time of his life, and I believe he was serious."

"Wow," I said, actually shocked that anyone could enjoy prison. But that explained why he hadn't wanted me to bail him out.

"Indeed," said Charles. "Well, once he was released, he tried to go straight. One of the inmates he'd befriended had a brother who owned a limousine company, and he got a job there washing and maintaining the cars. He got married again and had another kid, a daughter, and eventually he was promoted to a driver. But he was spending all of his money on Disney tattoos and memorabilia, when his wife wanted him to save for his daughter's college. And keep in mind he's still paying child support for his other two kids! Well, to pay the bills he started selling hash again. Then he moved onto acid and coke, and eventually to crack and heroin. At that point he was selling almost exclusively to Cast Members."

"There are Cast Members hooked on crack and heroin?!" I asked.

"Oh, you better believe it!" replied Charles.

"Walt would not approve."

"No, sir. And Jay's second wife didn't approve, either. It didn't take long before she got sick of drugged up people coming and going at all hours of the night, especially since her family was still living on the edge of poverty. Because the money was going right back into Jay's memorabilia habit! So she divorced him. The daughter stayed with him for a while, until I suppose she no longer thought his Disney obsession was 'cool', and then she left to live with her mother.

"I think this is where he hit rock bottom again, although according to him he was doing just fine. As he likes to tell it, a fairy came down and whispered into his ear the recipe for a special potion that would help a lot of people. It's a lot of hogwash, if you ask me. I think he got the recipe while he was in prison. Regardless, he stopped selling all of the other stuff and started cooking up batches of this new drug.

"It's truly amazing stuff, Blaine! It makes the world seem like a wonderland where nothing bad happens and everything is perfect and… well, I know it's clichéd, but it makes everything seem 'magical'."

"Is this that 'dust' stuff that I heard them talking about?" I asked.

"Yes! He calls it 'The Dust'. And the way it sparkles… it's glorious."

"I guess this is where you enter the story?" I asked, finishing my drink.

"Yes, sir," said Charles. "Another for the boy, and another for me, too!" he shouted to the bartender.

"Much appreciated," I said.

"You're going to need it for this next part," said Charles.

The bartender came over with another wonderful gin and tonic and I took a big gulp. Charles sipped his Scotch carefully.

"Proceed, kind benefactor!" I said.

"Well," continued Charles, "It was a little over two years ago when I first met Jay, and I'd been employed at Walt Disney World for fourteen years. I'd worked my way up from janitor at EPCOT Center to valet at The Beach Club. So I'd see him every day as he brought people to the hotel in his limo. Eventually we got to talking, and I felt he was a very nice gentleman. We were going through divorces at the same time, and I was having trouble dealing with mine. They'd promoted me to Greeter the day my divorce was finalized, and I just didn't know if I could do it. I didn't know if I could smile for all those lovely people all day and then go home and be okay with being completely alone."

He paused. I sipped my drink.

"You see, Blaine," said Charles, "the secret is that you don't need The Dust in the parks. Oh, no, you don't need The Dust here at all. It's when you're not in the parks, when you're home alone thinking about all the things that are wrong with your life… that's when you start to feel like the world out there is too complicated and sad and scary to deal with. That's when you need The Dust."

"So you started taking it? The Dust?"

"I did, indeed. And like I said, it was truly wonderful. It made me be able to go home and feel just like I do here. Like kids were smiling at me all day! I was all alone, but I didn't care. I had The Dust!"

"Yeah, that's the way people were talking about it at the party last night."

"A party, you say? Was Miss Nancy there?"

"Yeah, she was!" I said, surprised.

"Fine, fine woman, that Miss Nancy," said Charles. "I do miss seeing her. We sort of had a… thing."

"What?!"

"Oh, it was just for one night. Her husband had died, my wife had divorced me, we were both at Jay's on The Dust, and… well, one thing led to another, and…."

"Oh. My. God. I totally didn't need to know that. The mental image is horrifying. Damn you, Charles!"

He let out a loud guffaw, and then sighed. "Well, glad to know the old lady is still kicking, at least. Too bad she's still on The Dust, though."

"I think she can afford it, Charles. Supposedly she's filthy rich."

"True, but the others aren't. And the rub is, Jay is the only person who has it. He has the market cornered! And that made him a very wealthy man for a while. Of course, he blew it all on Disney memorabilia and tattoos, on top of alimony for two wives and child support for three kids. Didn't save a dime, as far as I know.

"But the real problem with him not having a financial cushion was that he was always at the mercy of the supplier of his secret ingredient. Some child labor camp in China, from what I could gather. Which is yet another reason why the whole enterprise is terrible. Anyway, the price of this one particular ingredient would fluctuate wildly, and as a result the price of The Dust often increased exponentially."

"That explains a lot," I said, thinking about Jay's argument with Lisa.

"And believe me, he's putting a hefty markup on it, because he needs that money for his own fix. He'd swear up and down that he wasn't doing The Dust himself. And it's true! But for him, getting tattoos and buying more Disney merchandise served the same purpose as The Dust did for the rest of us. A momentary thrill, a short escape from reality. He should have just done The Dust. It would have been a lot cheaper.

"Anyway, it was two days after I'd reached my fifteen-year anniversary here at Walt Disney World. There was a big ceremony and they gave me an incredible brass statue of Cinderella Castle, with my name engraved on it. I'd never been so proud, because I'd never stuck with anything that long! And I was great at the job. My managers knew it and appreciated me for it, and that statue was a symbol of everything good that I'd accomplished in my life.

"After the ceremony that evening I went to buy my regular fix of The Dust, and the price was too high. It'd risen twenty times at least since the previous week. I couldn't afford it. So I tried to quit the stuff, but after two sleepless nights I came crawling back to him.

"'I don't have the cash, but I'll give you anything,' I told him.

"'I want your fifteen-year Cast Member statue,' he said. 'I don't have one of those in my collection.'"

"Well, that tore my heart out. But I needed The Dust. In exchange for the statue he gave me what two weeks before would have been $50 worth of The Dust. He promised me that I could buy the statue back from him later. But he lied. He lied!"

Charles pounded his fist on the table. My gin and tonic sloshed violently. I picked it up and took a big gulp.

"In just a few months I saved up over a thousand dollars to pay him for that statue, which wasn't bad considering I was still buying The Dust and paying alimony. But when I handed it to him, he said it wasn't enough. I asked how much, and he said he'd know when I offered him the right amount. Well, I couldn't keep saving and buying The Dust, and keep paying alimony. So I decided right then and there that I was going to get my statue back, and that I was going to quit The Dust."

"And?" I asked. "Did you quit?"

"I did. I've been clean for nearly a year. Now, mind you, the drinking helps," he said, raising his glass and taking a sip. "But I've been going to therapy, too, and that also helps a lot. And more importantly, I've made amends with my wife and have just about forgiven myself for the way I treated her. We're not getting back together, but at least I'm just about ready to maybe start over again with someone else. I've had my eye on this cutie in the gift shop for a while now."

"Charles, you dog!" I said. "But wait. What happened with the statue?"

"He won't sell it back to me!" said Charles. "The bastard won't sell it, no matter how high a price I offer. I tried to give him ten thousand and he turned it down!"

"Well, I imagine that in a few weeks you might be able to buy it back for a lot less than that."

"How so?"

"I think Jay is going through some more rough times with his supplier." I said. "But this time you're not at his mercy. This time you'll be the one with the upper hand."

Charles frowned. "I'm sorry to hear about Jay," he said. "I wouldn't wish bad luck on anybody. But all I want is my statue back. I'm willing to pay him good money for it, and I don't see why he needs to hit rock bottom before he'll accept my payment. Blaine, next time you see him, please try to convince him to give that statue back to me?"

"Will do, Charles," I said, swallowing the last bit of my gin and tonic. "Thanks for the drinks."

"You're welcome. Just be sure to watch your back around that man. When people hit the bottom there's no telling what they'll do."

15

—That night I got up the nerve to go back into the Concierge Lounge. What did I care if Semi-Hot Sandra thought I was a creep? Fucking Snow White had tried to seduce me, and Semi-Hot Sandra had nothing on her. So, yeah, definitely her loss, I thought, as I sauntered past her.

"Hello, Mr. McKinnon!" she said gleefully.

"Hi, Semi…. Uh, Sandra," I said. I started laughing at my slip-up as I walked over to the bar area and poured a glass of wine.

Semi-Hot Sandra came up beside me. "What's so funny, Mr. McKinnon?" she asked, obviously afraid I was laughing at her. Which, I guess I was.

"Oh, nothing," I said, still chuckling. I surveyed the empty lounge, and took a seat on one of the sofas, facing a television that was showing my favorite Resort Channel video: Tracey in pigtails going down water slides.

Semi-Hot Sandra sat down next to me.

"How has your stay been so far, Mr…."

I cut her off. "Please, Sandra, please call me Blaine. For some reason when you call me Mr. McKinnon it makes me feel like a dirty old man."

"Oh. Okay, Blaine." she said, obviously taken aback. I didn't give a shit.

"My stay has been… interesting so far, Sandra."

"Have you been enjoying the parks?" she said, perking up a bit.

"Actually, I haven't even been to MGM or Animal Kingdom yet. Maybe I'll do MGM tomorrow."

I stared at the television. Pigtailed Tracey had nothing on Lisa, either. Nobody did. Lisa was maybe the hottest girl I'd ever seen.

"Yes, MGM is quite the park," prattled Semi-Hot Sandra. "Rock 'n' Roller Coaster is probably the best rollercoaster in existence! I just love the beginning, when it shoots…."

I turned slowly to her. "Sandra, I think I'd just like to sit here quietly for a while. I've had a lot of crazy shit happen to me over the past few days. I saw Princess Leia's tits and she asked me to cum on them."

Her mouth dropped open.

"I know!" I said. "Then I watched a nice old lady snort a line of drugs while a couple with a towel baby looked on, waiting their turn."

She stood up, staring at me in disgust.

"A naked tattooed man accosted Snow White and got arrested. And then a highly respected Cast Member told me story so outlandish that I still don't know if I believe it all."

She started backing away.

"So after all of that excitement, I was sorta hoping I could drink a few glasses of wine and just kinda chill for a bit."

"You're a very, very crude and abnormal man, Mr. McKinnon," she said, walking back to the Front Desk.

"Abnormal? Ah, whatever," I said. "You know you want me."

"Well, I never!" I heard her say as she turned the corner.

"Fucking prude," I muttered. But, in all honesty, I probably would have had reacted the same way if someone had told me all of that shit just a few days ago.

"I'm sorry, Sandra!" I yelled. No response.

So, I sipped my wine, watched Tracey running around the parks in tight pants, and tried my damnedest to digest the events of the past two days into some sort of palatable series of memories that would fit into the framework of my emotionally stunted existence. But my thoughts and feelings were all jangled up and strange.

More crazy shit had happened over the past 48 hours than had happened in the entirety of my previously sheltered life. It was like I'd entered a parallel dimension, like in one of those bad episodes of *Star Trek* where Spock has a beard or some crap like that.

And, I guess in a way this really was a new and exciting world for me to explore. Even with all the terrible stuff that had gone down.... I sorta liked it.

I felt alive.

16

—The next day I didn't hear anything from either Jay or Lisa. I figured Jay would be fine, but if Lisa was really getting off The Dust.... I kicked myself for not getting her number. She didn't have mine, either. But she knew my name, and she knew where I was staying, so she could always call the Front Desk and have them transfer her to my room.

So, like a jackass, I sat around the room for two days, waiting for her to call.

I had some books sent up from the gift shop downstairs, but they were all snoozers and my mind was constantly drifting back to Lisa. Was she okay? Did she have feelings for me? Had she really left Jay for good? Had she enjoyed kissing me as much as I'd enjoyed kissing her? Then I'd start thinking about the way she smelled and tasted, and I'd nearly go crazy just wanting to see her again.

It was driving me nuts, and I needed to take my mind off of her. So I asked the Concierge to send up some really trashy Paparazzi rags, ordered some Giordano's Chicago-Style deep dish, and sat in my Jacuzzi for two days eating pizza, drinking beer, and enjoying the misfortunes of celebrities.

Poring over those magazines, it occurred to me that these people's lives weren't so different than mine had been lately. Stories of rich dipshits, drugs, love triangles, arrests, eccentric personalities.... Except it was funny when that crap happened to them. Which, in a weird way, sorta gave me some perspective on everything that had happened to me, and made me feel better. At least there was the possibility that I could eventually look back on all of this and laugh.

The next day I left the room, and decided to head to MGM Studios. Lisa could leave a message.

I decided to walk there, past The BoardWalk, and down a path that ran along the canal that the Friendship Boats sailed along. The weather was perfect, and the walk was calm and relaxing.

Cute little lizards were everywhere, sunning themselves and scrambling whenever I walked past them. I remembered as a kid, girls used to catch the lizards, somehow get them to bite their ears, and then walk around wearing them like earrings. I also remembered how if you held them by their tails for too long, the tails would separate from their bodies. The lizard would scurry off and you'd be left holding its wiggling appendage. Then over the next few weeks you'd catch sight of that same lizard, its lost limb slowly growing back.

Then I remembered how once when I was a little kid, I'd purposely stepped on one of these cute, harmless lizards, crushing it and killing it. I don't know why I did it. Kids have a streak of curious cruelty, I think. Anyway, the carcass laid there for weeks, a little bit of its intestines squeezed out of its mouth. The ants stripped it bare after a while, and it turned into a skeleton. I remembered walking by it every day, knowing that I'd killed it, and feeling so horribly guilty. I imagined that maybe the little lizard had baby lizards, and I worried that I'd killed their mother, and now the babies would starve to death or something.

And then thinking about the dead lizard brought up memories of Sam, hanging there with his intestines draped to the ground. And me looking at him, wondering how anyone could do something so cruel to an innocent animal. But I'd done nothing less to that lizard. Did it matter that Sam was much bigger than that little lizard? They were both living things with the ability to feel pain. Did size dictate the morality of killing something?

I wondered if Ricky Lu felt as guilty about what he did to Sam as I felt about that lizard? I hoped so. I hoped it was tearing him apart. Probably not, though. Asshole.

I finally passed through the turnstiles of MGM Studios. I walked down the main avenue, a recreation of 40s-era Hollywood, and turned right onto Sunset Boulevard. I smelled something that made my mouth water, and spied a turkey leg stand. I hadn't eaten breakfast, so I instinctively bought one and eagerly chomped down on it. I tore into that turkey leg, breaking through the muscle and fat. And when I pulled it away from my mouth it was bright pink and there were little blood vessels hanging from the meat.

With Sam and the lizard still fresh on my mind, I couldn't help but make the obvious connection.

I spit out the meat, disgusted.

Minutes earlier I'd been beating myself up about killing a lizard over twenty-five years ago, and hoping the man who had murdered my dog was wracked with guilt. Yet here I was eating a dead animal who for all I knew was just as loving and smart as Sam. And a goddamned turkey was certainly smarter than a lizard.

I was about to throw the foul thing in the trash, but then felt bad about wasting it. I didn't know what to do with it, though. It was seriously grossing me out. But who the hell was going to want a turkey leg that had a bite taken out of it?

Theresa Skywalker, that's who.

I saw her following a parade float, screaming at the characters onboard. What was actually a moving stage stopped in front of the giant blue Sorcerer's hat from *Fantasia,* which now completely blocked the previously scenic view of Grauman's Chinese Theater.

Theresa was wearing a skimpy cheerleading uniform which matched those of the girls on the stage. She was swinging around pom-poms and perfectly mimicking all of their cheerleading moves.

She kept screaming, "I love you, Troy Bolton!"

What the fuck was this nonsense?

"*High School Musical* Pep Rally," read the signage on the float.

"Seriously, Theresa?" I asked as I came up behind her.

"Blaine!" she shouted, nearly knocking my head off with a pom-pom.

The show ended and the cast posed for pictures with the crowd. Theresa jammed a camera into my hands and pushed herself to the front of Troy's line. She stood next to him, grinning, as I snapped the picture. Then she whispered something into his ear which made him gasp, and then blush, and then smile slyly. I can only imagine she was asking him to cum on her tits.

"Hi Blaine!" she said cheerfully, taking back her camera. "Isn't Troy a dreamboat?"

"He sure is," I said.

"I think we're going to hang out later!"

"What will Luke think? And what happened to Ron Stoppable?"

"They're both holding out on me. I need some serious deep dicking, Blaine!"

I laughed, and then laughed some more at the fact that her lewd pronouncement hadn't shocked me at all.

"Here, take this," I said, handing her the turkey leg.

"Oh, thank you!" she said. She looked at it and frowned. "There's already a bite taken out of it."

"I know, that was from me."

She crinkled her nose.

"I just decided I didn't want it," I said, pushing it at her.

She still wasn't convinced, but I was determined that this turkey hadn't died for naught!

"It's got my saliva on it, so if you eat it, it'll almost be like we're making out."

Her eyes lit up, and she snatched the turkey leg. She then proceeded to lick the place where I'd bitten it, and then sucked on it, and then licked it some more. She was giving the turkey leg a blowjob. It was at once horribly disgusting and extremely hot.

"Whoa, cool it down, Theresa! Save it for Troy!" I said.

"I can fuck both of you!" she said loudly. Mothers turned their heads toward her and covered their children's ears.

"Yeah, yeah, I suppose you could, in theory. But I'm sorta holding out for Lisa, and I don't think she'd be too happy if I let you... lick my turkey leg."

"You and Lisa?!" she squealed.

"Yeah, I think so," I said, hesitating. "We kinda had a thing the other night, and she left Jay, and...."

Theresa stopped me. "She left Jay?"

I nodded.

"Well, how's she going to get...." She trailed off.

"The Dust?" I asked, finishing her sentence.

"Yeah, The Dust."

"She's quitting it. She's not doing it anymore."

"Oh. That's not good." She looked at the ground and shuffled her feet.

"Is there something you need to tell me, Theresa?"

"It's just that... everyone takes The Dust for a reason, Blaine. I mean, I take it because I'm socially awkward and have trouble interacting with real people. The characters here get paid to talk to me and they have to at least pretend that they like me. People in the real world don't have to do that. They're usually mean to me, actually. Without The Dust I'd probably never leave the house except to come here. I wouldn't even be able to interact with the cashier at the grocery store. It helps me act like a normal person."

I looked at her in her cheerleading outfit and snickered.

"You know what I mean!" she said, hitting me on the shoulder.

"Anyway, you can't just stop unless you're willing to deal with the things that made you start taking it to begin with," she said.

I thought about Charles telling me how he'd gone to therapy and reconciled with his wife. And how he'd also turned to booze as a crutch to help him through the bad times. I wondered what Lisa's crutch would be?

"So, what made Lisa start taking it?" I asked.

"We never really talked about it," she said. "It's sort of bad manners to talk about that kind of stuff when you're on The Dust. But she'd let little things out every once in a while." She stopped.

"Do you really want to hear this?"

"I don't know. Maybe not."

But, on the off-chance Lisa finally called, I wouldn't be much help if I didn't understand what she was dealing with.

"Yeah, I guess I need to know," I said. "But I'm going to need a drink first."

Theresa Skywalker/Stoppable/Bolton jumped up and down.

"I want an alcoholic milkshake at The Tune-In Lounge!"

"Okay, sounds good," I said. "Finish your turkey leg."

She devoured it as we walked to the bar area of The 50s Prime Time Café, a re-creation of a 50s house, where "Mom" cooked and your "Cousins" served you. They played old sitcoms like *I Love Lucy* on mini TVs mounted to each table. I hated the place as a kid because the waiters would always scold me for not cleaning my plate. It was all in jest, but I didn't get that as a kid, and my parents laughing at the whole situation just made it worse.

But man, they sure made a mean alcoholic milkshake.

Even better, at one point "Cousin" the bartender said, "You better finish that whole thing, or Mom will be angry!"

To which I replied, "Go fuck yourself, Cousin," and relished the shocked look on his face. It was awesome retribution for my childhood torment. But then I felt bad, because he was just a Cast Member being paid to perform this role, so I left him a $100 tip.

"Thank you, Cousin!" he yelled.

I rolled my eyes and turned to Theresa.

"So what's the story?" I asked, as she finished her milkshake.

"What's the story, morning glory, what's the word, hummingbird?" she sang.

What a weirdo.

"Seriously, Theresa. What's Lisa's deal?"

"Like I said, I don't really know much," she said, and then started loudly sucking the remains of her milkshake through a straw. She stopped, and then started doing it again.

"Theresa!" I shouted.

"Geesh, Blaine."

"I can get you another one, if you want."

"No, I don't want another one."

"Then please stop being annoying, and tell me about Lisa's... deep, dark secrets, or whatever you think you have on her."

"I dunno. I just remember overhearing her talking to Jay once about some cult she was in, and her father was the leader. And then the police came in and tried to make them all leave. But there was a fire and her mother and father were killed. And she was on TV, and...."

"Wait, a minute. Wait, wait, wait, wait. Was this here in Orlando?"

"Yeah, I think that's what she said."

"You're shitting me, right?"

"No, why?"

"I totally remember the chemical engineers talking about this when I was working at Goddard! This destitute cult was cooped up in that crazy Xanadu House of the Future. The whole thing was basically made out of Styrofoam, and when the cops shot the tear gas in there it ignited an oil tank and the oil mixed with the Styrofoam and turned the building into a big ball of napalm! I heard the fire burned for weeks."

"I don't really know what you're talking about," said Theresa.

"Holy shit." I thought for a second. "She's twenty-three, so that means she would have been... ten years old when it happened. Wow."

I sat there, totally knocked for a loop. Theresa noisily sucked on her milkshake again.

"Hey!" I yelled.

"What?!" yelled Theresa Skywalker.

"Her number?"

Theresa shook her head in confusion.

"Her phone number. Lisa's phone number? Do you have it?"

"Sure," she said, pulling out her cell phone. "This is it right here."

I copied it into my phone and jumped off my stool.

"Thanks, Theresa. Good luck with Troy. I hope he gives you what you're looking for."

"You mean a serious deep dicking?"

"No, sweetheart. But good luck with that, too."

I ran out of the park, stopping only to pick up a lizard who was seconds away from being snatched from the sidewalk by a dive-bombing crow. I kissed its little head and it latched onto my lower lip. The son of a bitch wouldn't let go. So I ran the rest of the way with the lizard on my lip.

"Hi, Charles," I said as I ran through the lobby, and smiled, the lizard still dangling from my lip.

Charles shook his head. "You got problems, son," he said as I bolted into the elevator.

When I got into the room I went to the wet bar's mirror and gently pulled the lizard off my lip. I cupped him in my hand and set him outside on the balcony to sun himself, and then came back inside and popped open my laptop. I spent hours reading everything I could about the Xanadu cult and watching news footage of the fire on YouTube. There were a few clips where a little girl who looked like Lisa was shown running out of the house, alone, into the arms of a SWAT officer. It had to be her. I watched it over and over. The footage was heartbreaking.

But even worse were the reports from a few of the others who'd escaped before the fire. They all said that the leader of the cult, who I guess was Lisa's dad, was having sex with kids as young as ten. Was there really someone sick enough to have sex with his own ten year old daughter? Despite my newfound love of life, I had no problem admitting that a fiery death wasn't nearly bad enough for such an asshole.

Once I felt I had an emotional grasp on the whole thing, I decided to call her. Predictably, it went to voicemail.

"Hey, Lisa, it's Blaine," I said.

I hated leaving voice messages. Was anyone actually good at talking to a faceless machine? EPCOT Center should have had an exhibit about how to leave decent voicemails.

"Um, I got your number from Theresa Skywalker." I paused. "I didn't cum on her tits, I just ran into her at MGM. Anyway, I'm really worried about you getting off of The Dust. She told me about the Xanadu house, and... well, that's some fucked up shit. At the very least, can you call me back and let me know you're okay? I know that sounds really selfish considering what you're probably going through right now, but... you know I care for you. A lot. Which, considering we've only known each other for a few days is kinda odd, but it seemed like you felt the same way, and.... Shit, this is turning into one of those disastrous voice messages like they always have in stupid romantic comedies and cheesy sitcoms. Okay, well, anyway, call me back at this number if you want to talk. I.... Okay, bye."

That was awful. I pressed the pound key and told it not to send the message.

Should I tell her I loved her? We'd spent less than twenty-four hours together. Seemed more than weird to tell someone I knew less than a day that I loved them. But... maybe that's what she needed? Shit, I didn't know what to say.

But I knew somebody who did.

I ran downstairs to the lobby.

"Charles!" I yelled.

He came through the front sliding doors, looking dapper as ever, leading a family of six to the check-in desk.

I waited, shuffling around like I had to pee, as he gave them his full attention. He bent down and gave all of the kids pins, saluted the parents, and finally turned towards me.

"You're so good at this job," I said. "I really admire that."

"Thank you, kind sir!" he said. "Now, what can I do you for?"

"Charles, you're maybe the only person who can help me here." I lowered my voice. "Lisa, the girl who used to be with Jay, left him and is quitting The Dust."

Charles smiled and firmly pushed me towards the elevator.

"Let me show you to your floor, Mr. McKinnon!"

We stepped into the elevator and he did his same trick with

the key.

"This better be good, Mr. McKinnon. You can't be talking to me about The Dust while I'm on the job!"

"Shit, sorry. Yeah, that was really inconsiderate," I said. "But I didn't know who else to talk to. You've been there, you know what it feels like to get off the stuff. See, this girl, Lisa, I think I'm in love with her. I mean, we've only known each other for a few days, but I think she left Jay because of me, but now she won't call me back because she's detoxing from The Dust, and I tried to leave her a message but I didn't know if I should tell her I loved her because I didn't know what the detox was like, and if she'd really like it or really hate it if she knew...." I took a deep breath. "If she knew that I was in love with her."

Charles stared at me. The alarm started going off, and he released the key and pushed the button for the fifth floor. The elevator rose.

"Mr. McKinnon, do you truly love this girl? Or are you just maybe just high on the idea of loving her? Because if you're just high on the idea, well, now that'd be one more junkie in her life feeding off a reality that doesn't exist. And I don't see how that'd be of much help to her, regardless of how much she'd probably like to hear that someone out there truly loves her."

It felt like someone had sucker punched me.

The elevator door opened, and I stepped out.

"Tell her you're there for her if she needs you, son. If I'd had someone telling me that when I was coming off The Dust, well, maybe I'd still have that statue of mine."

The door closed.

I went back to my room and dialed Lisa's number.

"Lisa, it's Blaine. I want you to know that I'm here for you. If you need anything, anything at all, let me know. Hope you're okay. Bye."

I hung up, letting the message go through. Charles was right. That was totally the way to go. I couldn't be telling someone I loved them when I'd never been in love before. I didn't know what the hell love was. But it probably wasn't what I was feeling now. What I felt now seemed more like... well, like a drug, just like Charles said.

Damn, that old man was smart.

17

—Lisa never did call me back. Eventually I stopped checking my phone every minute, no longer worried I'd missed a call.

But then about two weeks later I did get a call, one that I'd sorta hoped I wouldn't receive. It was Jay.

"Hey, Blaine," he said.

"Hey, Jay. What's going on, buddy?"

"I'm in a bit of a pickle here, and it looks like I need to leave my house. I haven't paid the mortgage for a few months, and they're finally evicting me."

"Damn, dude. What can I do?"

"Could you help me move all of my memorabilia into storage? Anything left in the house is going to be taken by the bank tomorrow."

"Yeah, absolutely," I said. "You wanna come pick me up now?"

Silence.

"Jay? I'm here at The Beach Club. Come pick me up!"

"I don't have the limo anymore, Blaine."

"Oh."

"I lost the job the day after I was arrested, as expected."

"Um, okay. Look, that's cool. I'll get a cab to Home Depot, rent one of their trucks, and…." I stopped, realizing what I was saying.

My parents. Fucking hell.

"Blaine?"

"Yeah. Sorry. Yeah, I'll get one of their trucks and drive over to your house. We'll get it all in one trip and drive it to a storage place. No problem. See you in a few hours?"

"Thanks, Blaine. You're a good friend."

"You bet," I said. Little did he know that I was less a good friend than I was a big sack of guilt. I still felt like this was all my fault.

I caught a cab out front of The Beach Club, and told the driver to bring me to the nearest Home Depot. I rented a truck, got behind the wheel, and stared at the interior of the cab.

This truck had killed my parents. Well, not this truck, but one like it. And not really the truck itself, but the dumbass driving the truck.

I turned the key, stepped on the gas, and jerked backwards, immediately hearing a screeching of tires, a blaring horn, and yelling.

Holy fuck, I'd already killed someone.

I opened the door and looked back only to see a douchebag in a red Miata speed off, shaking his fist at me. I hadn't seen him because he was doing nearly sixty down the crowded parking lot aisle.

"Slow down, asshole!" I yelled, as he tore through the lot, the gust from his car nearly knocking over an old lady.

Why were all dudes who drove Miatas either gay (nothing wrong with that), or 'roided out douchebag gym rats (definitely something wrong with that)?

I got back into the truck, now all jacked up on adrenaline, slowly pulled out of the parking spot, and started driving.

I completely freaked as I started braking at the first red light I hit.

"This must have been the same view that guy had right before he slammed into my parents' car," I thought frantically. "Everything seems okay, and then all of a sudden you're on top of the car in front of you, and a lady is decapitated and a man is bleeding to death and cursing about monorails."

But the brakes worked as they were supposed to, and I came to a full and complete stop.

I'd never even met the guy who was driving the truck. I wondered what his life ended up being like, and if he still thought about my parents? Had he been able to deal with the guilt, or had he turned to something like The Dust?

I hoped not.

Because I was quickly coming to understand that bad shit happened to everyone, and a lot of it was stuff we didn't have any control over. Just random tragedy, doled out to any unlucky sucker who happened to be in the wrong place at the wrong time. And maybe it was how we dealt with getting shit on by the universe that revealed the type of person we were deep inside? If that was the case, I was a big fucking pussy straight to the core, because I kept running away whenever I drew the short straw....

I put my philosophical musings aside as I turned the truck into Jay's subdivision. Driving up to his house, I was shocked to see nearly all of his belongings lined up neatly on his driveway. He was standing watch over them, sleeveless shirt tucked into jean shorts, as usual. I pulled the truck alongside the curb so the back lined up with the end of his driveway. I jumped out of the cab and greeted him.

"You ready for some heavy lifting, fatty?" I said, smacking him on the shoulder. He wasn't amused.

"Please be careful with it all, Blaine. I don't know what I'd do if even a single piece was damaged. These things," he said, waving his arms around the boxes, "they're my life. Each one is a piece of me."

"C'mon, Jay. The *Little Mermaid* soap dish is a piece of you?" I said, laughing.

He didn't smile.

"Okay," I said. "Fair enough."

We spent the next five hours carefully loading all of Jay's possessions into the truck. There were some really heavy things that were difficult to load, like the bar and the Mutoscope viewer, but really it was a job that should have taken an hour. Unfortunately, he slowed the whole process down immensely by being extremely anal about the placement of the boxes, triple-checking that every box was fully balanced and wasn't crushing anything beneath.

Nevertheless, despite his best efforts, we'd just about finished loading the truck when he accidentally backed into column of boxes, causing one to fall from about four feet up. I heard something break. Jay freaked out, tore open the box, and pulled out a piece of a shattered coffee mug. It was the EPCOT Center mug that I'd been drinking from the morning after my unfortunate airport arrival.

He just sat there, staring at the broken mug. Then he started crying, sobbing uncontrollably. I didn't know what to do.

"Hey, it's cool, Jay. I've seen those on eBay for like twenty bucks. We can get another one by next week."

No response. He ended up sitting in that truck for an hour, crying over a goddamned coffee mug. I mean, I felt bad, but it was just all sorts of crazy.

"I'll be in the house if you need me," I said.

It was weird seeing his place looking like a normal house. What had once been a magical museum had reverted back to a regular Florida rancher. It was depressing.

He'd left any non-Disney furniture behind, although a lot of it had obviously been stripped of various customizations he'd made. The feet on pretty much everything, for example, from his bed to his armoire to his kitchen table, used to be yellow plastic Mickey feet. Those had all been removed. The doors on his entertainment center had been custom made from two different colors of wood, the darker wood in the middle forming a Mickey head. The doors had been taken off their hinges. Every light switch plate was gone, because they'd all been Disney-themed. The handles on all of the sinks, which had been white Mickey hands, had been removed. Toilet paper holders, all gone. Custom-painted toilet seats? Gone. He'd even removed the non-slip pads in the bathtub because they were Little Mermaid-shaped rubber stickers of some sort. Craziest of all, a large section of tiles which had been custom painted with a *Mickey Mouse Club* logo was missing from his foyer. He'd actually removed ceramic tiles from the floor! I couldn't even imagine how long that had taken him to do without breaking any of them. Or maybe he had broken them and then sat there crying about it for a day.

I went out to his garage, which I'd never been in before. It had a really odd smell to it, like sweet chemicals. There were different types of gas tanks in one corner, and industrial-sized buckets of really random stuff, like bleach and baking soda. Obviously this was his Dust lab.

And sure enough, sitting on a workbench was the only Disney item left in the entire house: a replica of The Queen's dagger-through-the-heart box from *Snow White*. I walked over and opened it. Inside was a small notepad, and nothing else. I picked it up and turned to the first page. All that was written were the words "Pixie Dust Recipe".

"Please put that down, Blaine," said Jay.

I spun around to see him standing in the garage doorway. He walked over, grabbed the notepad, and threw it back into the box.

"Sorry, Jay. I was just doing a final check of the house, and it looked like you'd accidentally left this behind."

"How much did you see?" he asked, slightly frantic. "Did you see the secret ingredient?"

"No, dude. Just the first page."

He stared at me. I shrugged.

"Okay," he said, grabbing the box from the shelf. "Trust me, Blaine. There are some things it's best you didn't know." He shook the box. "This is one of them."

"Jay, I know all about The Dust."

"No. No, you have no idea. The secret ingredient? The one I can't get anymore because it's too expensive? It's horrible. It's the most disgusting thing, Blaine. You don't want to know. I have to carry the guilt around with me every second of my life, and there's no reason for anyone else to have to share that burden. If any of them knew what they'd been taking, what The Dust was made of.... Blaine, I truly believe they'd all kill themselves."

"Christ, Jay." I shook my head.

"That's why I've never done it. I wish I could. Maybe if I did The Dust I wouldn't need to keep all that stuff out there." He motioned to the truck wearily, and then sat on a bucket of bleach.

"You know, there's probably a million dollars worth of memorabilia in that truck? And I can't even bring myself to sell a ten dollar faucet handle! I understand I'm not right in the head, but that doesn't change anything. It's just that each trinket, each collectible, no matter how big or small, has some memory attached to it. And selling it would be like destroying that memory. They're all little pieces of my life."

"Dude, just go to therapy. Charles said it worked great for him."

He shook his head.

"You should really get back in touch with your dad, too," I continued, undeterred. "Having that whole situation hanging over your head can't be healthy."

"My dad is dead."

"No, he's not."

"I don't want to talk about him."

"That's my point. That right there is a perfect reason why you need to go to therapy."

"Blaine, I don't have the money for therapy, and even if I did… well, I'd spend it on the ingredient for The Dust and then buy some more Disney stuff."

"That's great, Jay. So you tell me that, and now I feel like an ass for giving you three hundred the other day. You know I can't give you any more cash now, right?"

"Yeah, I know."

"Okay, fair enough."

I looked at him, sitting on a bleach bucket, all down and out and feeling sorry for himself. He'd helped me more than a few times. I still owed him. Plus, he was my friend.

"I tell you what I can do for you, though," I said. "I can give you a place to crash until you get back on your feet."

"At The Beach Club?" he said, and smiled for the first time that day.

"Yeah, man, living it up in style at The Beach Club! And since you're my guest you'll have full access to the Concierge Lounge, so you can eat and drink all you want there."

"Wow, really?!"

"Really," I said.

I paused, frowning.

"What is it?" he asked.

"Can you do one favor for me in return?" I asked. "Can you give Charles his statue back?"

His face contorted. He didn't speak for a while.

"I don't think so," he said, finally. "Not right now, anyway. Maybe once everything calms down and I'm feeling a little better. But not now."

"Dude, I'm asking you for one favor! It's not even your goddamned statue! You basically stole it from Charles. How could that possibly have any good memories associated with it?"

He dropped his head down and wrapped his hands around the back of his neck.

"Jay!" I said. "What the hell?"

"It was Lisa's favorite piece in the whole house!" he said, jerking his head back up. "She used to lay in our bed, staring at it for hours on the nightstand. She said that Castle was her dream home."

"Ah, whatever, dude. You should've just bought her a playset or something. Did she know that it you'd fucking stolen it from somebody?"

"She didn't know I took it from Charles, no. I didn't have the heart to tell her. She said it was like a carrot on a stick that motivated her not to fall back into her old lifestyle, and to stay normal and stable enough to someday have her own home, her own castle."

"Damn," I said. "What does that mean, 'her old lifestyle'?"

"Those tattoos didn't just magically appear, Blaine. She had a completely different life when she was a teenager, before she started working at Disney. She's been through some wild times."

"Yeah. Theresa Skywalker told me about the Xanadu cult. That's some fucked up shit."

"But that wasn't anywhere near the end of it. She bounced from foster home to foster home, was abused multiple times, and then ran away and was homeless for a while, and…. And then she got it together. I don't know what pushed her to do it, but she got a GED, saved up some money, and started taking care of herself. Got a job as a handler at The Magic Kingdom, eventually auditioned for a Face Character role, and, well, you know the rest."

"Wow."

"I miss her, Blaine. She's got a tough exterior, but on the inside she's still a scared little girl who needs to be protected and made to feel safe. I definitely failed at that job…." He trailed off. "Every time she did The Dust I wanted to puke. She seemed to need it so badly, but I just couldn't keep watching her do it. It was horrible. She said being in The Magic Kingdom was pretty close to the feeling she got from The Dust. But when the lights went down and the gates closed… that's when the panic and the depression and the cravings kicked in."

"Have you heard from her?" I asked.

"No. Nothing. You?"

"No. I called her and left a message, but she never called me back."

"She seemed to trust you."

"Apparently not enough to let me help."

Jay sighed. "Even though I don't expect she'll ever want to talk to me again, I really do hope she's going to be okay. I got her hooked on the stuff, and that's a heavy weight to carry."

He stood up, holding The Queen's box.

"Anyway, hopefully that explains why I can't give Charles his statue back. Not right now, anyway. Maybe once I'm over Lisa…. Maybe."

"He'll be less than thrilled," I said. "But, maybe I can make him understand. He's a cool guy, Jay."

"I know. We had some good times together. I'm glad he's off

The Dust and doing well for himself."

I stood up, too, drained physically and emotionally.

"Let's put the last few boxes in the truck and get the hell out of here," I said.

"We still have to unload everything at the storage facility."

"Holy shit," I said. I was about to drop from exhaustion. "Fuck that. We'll swing back by Home Depot and hire some of those day laborers to do it for us."

Jay started to object, but I cut him off.

"I'll pay for it. No way I'm lifting another goddamned box today."

So that's what we did. Jay loaded the last two boxes into the truck and got into the front seat, carrying The Queen's box and Charles' statue. We drove to Home Depot, him cringing every time we hit a bump in the road. A few guys were still standing outside, so I got out, gave them each a hundred, and they piled into the truck with us.

"Nice tattoos, mister," said the one sitting next to Jay.

"Thanks," he responded.

"You like Disney, eh?"

"It's my whole life," said Jay.

"I like Disney, too, but they won't hire me," He pointed to the tattoos on his knuckles.

"You know, they have makeup for that," said Jay.

"Aw, I can't afford that stuff," said the man. "And besides, if they don't want me the way I am, then I don't want to work there."

We drove the rest of the way in silence. The man's words looped in my brain, over and over again. He was right. Lisa shouldn't have to hide who she was, hide her past, to work at the place she loved. That was bullshit. Fuck Disney.

The two men took less than thirty minutes to unload everything into the air conditioned storage unit I'd rented for Jay.

"We're just keeping all this here until you get back on your feet," I said to Jay.

"Technically, it's all yours now," he stated. "You're the one paying the bill for the unit."

"I'll keep it here for you as long as you need me to."

"I really appreciate it, Blaine."

He hugged me, and I hugged him back.

"Let's go to The Beach Club, okay?" I said.

"Can't wait," said Jay.

We dropped off the two men and the truck and snagged a cab back to The Beach Club. Per Jay's request we avoided Charles by circling around the side of the resort and past the gift shop, instead of going through the front doors. He probably saw us anyway, though. Couldn't get anything past that dude.

We walked into the suite, and Jay nodded, smiling.

"Wow, this is amazing," he said.

"Yeah, it's pretty nice." I pointed to the couch. "So that's your bed. I think it folds out. I'll have to get you some blankets, though. There's a half bath over there. You can use my shower but wait until after I'm done with it in the morning. I'll let Semi-Hot Sandra know that you can use the Lounge...."

"Semi-Hot Sandra?"

I laughed. "Yeah. She's an ultra-prude. But she totally wants me."

Jay looked at me, confused, shook his head, and fell onto the couch. Within seconds he was snoring.

I guess I had a roommate.

—

I went downstairs to get a massively overpriced bottle of wine from the gift shop, so I could drink it in the Jacuzzi. I needed something to help me sleep after all the shit that had gone down that day.

Charles was hanging out in the lobby as I exited the gift shop. He was smiling at everyone who walked past, saluting some people and calling out to others by name. I walked over to him.

"Mr. McKinnon!" he said. "What a nice surprise!"

"Hey, Charles," I said.

"And what have you been up to today?"

"Oh, boy," I said. "Well, for one, I helped Jay move out of his house. He's living up in the room with me now."

"So he really did hit rock bottom."

"Yeah, that's for sure."

"Mr. McKinnon," Charles said, hesitating. "Did you by any chance talk to him about my statue?"

"We spent a really long time talking about it, actually," I said. "It's complicated."

"I just want my statue back."

"Yeah, I totally understand. But there's a lot more to it than just the statue. Jay has… serious issues. And that statue has come to mean a lot to him."

"It meant a lot to me, too," he said.

"Yeah… I know. It's… well, shit, there's no reason not to tell you. That was Lisa's favorite piece of memorabilia that Jay had at his house. She attached all sorts of emotional significance to it, and now that she's left Jay, well, he's attached all sorts of emotional significance to it."

"I see…" said Charles.

"So, like I said, it's complicated. He really thinks that every little Disney memento he has is like a piece of his soul or something crazy like that. Anyway, it did seem like he'd be more willing to part with it once he's over Lisa. That might take a while, though. I'm going to try to get him to go to therapy, too, so maybe that'll help."

Charles nodded, but didn't speak.

"He needs it more than you do right now, Charles."

"You're a good friend, Mr. McKinnon," he replied.

"Thanks for understanding," I said.

He patted me on the back. I nodded, and walked towards the elevators.

Jay was still snoring as I quietly opened the door to the suite and walked back in. Like a total weirdo I watched him sleep for a minute, and then went into my room and drank the whole bottle of wine.

It was strange, but also kinda cool, having someone else around all the time. I'd been living alone for so long that I figured even the annoying stuff about having a roommate, like someone snoring on my couch, for example, would be new and funny and, well… really nice.

We spent the next day sitting out on the balcony, me drinking gin and tonics, him drinking lemonade. A little lizard scattered across the concrete, over Jay's toes and up my leg.

"Ah!" said Jay, screaming like a girl. He grabbed a magazine, rolled it up, and was about to swat the lizard off my leg.

"Don't you dare," I said.

I looked down at the lizard, picked him up, and gave him a peck on his cute head. The little bastard latched onto my lip! It was the same one! I turned to Jay, the lizard dangling from my lip, and laughed at the horrified look on his face.

He hung from my lip for a good hour before deciding to move off to a better spot to sun himself. I loved that little guy. I decided to name him Bill, after the lizard in *Alice in Wonderland*.

Now I had a roommate and a pet. Things were looking up.

18

—Jay and I spent the next few weeks bumming around the parks, him showing me lots of cool backstage shit. All of the employees seemed to know him. People were always waving to him. I guess there was some sort of unspoken agreement that since he'd sold drugs, The Dust or otherwise, to so many Cast Members who were now high-level managers, he pretty much had the run of the property. Nobody wanted to risk having their past, or current, indiscretions exposed.

We rode bikes around the back of MGM – apparently any bike that's green is communal property that the Cast Members can use to quickly get back and forth between the expansive backstage there. That was a ton of fun until I accidentally biked onstage into the Streets of America and just about mowed down a family of five. We stopped riding the bikes after that.

Theresa Skywalker wasn't anywhere to be found at MGM. I was worried about her, so I talked to one of the cheerleaders after the *High School Musical* show, and it turned out that Troy Bolton was also MIA. So either she'd taken him hostage and was holding him as a sex slave in her basement, or, hopefully, the two were madly in love and would live happily ever after.

Jay seemed to know something that he wasn't telling me, because he wasn't the least bit concerned.

"Did Theresa Skywalker try to get more of The Dust before you were evicted, Jay?" I asked.

"She did come to see me," he said. "But it wasn't to buy The Dust. She was actually trying to sell some back to me."

"What?!"

"Oh, she was fine. It only took her a few days to kick it. She was never a heavy user, anyway. Sort of on and off. She'd meet a boy and obsess over him and I wouldn't see her for weeks, then the boy would leave her and she'd be back that day. Her self-esteem was quite low."

"So she was already off of it when she came to see you?"

"She was. She wouldn't stop talking about this Troy fellow. He'd been offered a six month job performing on one of the Disney cruise ships, and was going to bring her with him."

That cracked me up something fierce. I laughed so long that my stomach started hurting. Tears were streaming down my face. Jay looked on, clearly not amused.

"Holy shit," I said, sniffing and wiping my eyes. "Can you imagine six months cooped up on a cruise ship with Theresa Skywalker? You sure this guy wasn't on something, too?"

"Now, Blaine, be nice. She's a really sweet girl deep down. Just very, very insecure and awkward. Perhaps this Troy was a little more insightful than you're giving him credit for."

"I saw the dude. He looked kinda like a douchebag. Like someone who would drive a Miata."

"What's wrong with Miatas?" asked Jay.

Which, of course, set me off on another laughing fit.

"Well, regardless," he said, talking over my laughter, "as far as I know they're living on a cruise ship together. I'm sure we'll get a postcard from her first port of call."

"Either that, or he's already pushed her overboard," I said, still chuckling. "Nah, I shouldn't joke about that. I hope she's happy. I kinda regret not fucking her, though."

"Why didn't you?" asked Jay.

"Uh...." I stammered, thinking about the agreement I'd made with Lisa. Couldn't very well tell Jay about that. "Uh, it just wouldn't have been right. And I was afraid she'd stalk me if we hooked up. Yeah, that's why."

"She probably would have stalked you."

"Yeah," I said. But thinking about it, I actually was kinda pissed that I hadn't fucked Theresa Skywalker. It'd been years since I'd scored, and it certainly didn't look like it was going to happen with Lisa. I was such a tool.

The next day we circled the entirety of EPCOT Center's perimeter, entering the employee-only area via a small walkway to the left of Guest Services and continuing all the way to a door on the right side of the Main Gate, just past The Living Seas. We went into Costuming and got pictures of the two of us trying on silly Cast Member outfits. We passed the Illuminations barge, tied to a dumpy looking dock in a dirty lagoon. We saw the shell of a sub from the *20,000 Leagues Under the Sea* ride sitting in a field behind the area slotted for the unbuilt Equatorial Africa pavilion. Then we hopped on a Cast Member bus and rode it all the way to the Imagination pavilion, where we stopped to visit the maintenance bay for the ride vehicles. I briefly considered starting an axle grease fire and laughing like a maniac as the whole pavilion burned to the ground. But it wasn't the building's fault the ride sucked now.

The day after that we went to Animal Kingdom, where a manager took me and Jay on our own personal Kilimanjaro Safaris tour, driving down paths that the regular ride didn't use. A big stupid rhinoceros got in our way at one point. We honked and honked but the fucker wouldn't even acknowledge our presence. He finally dropped a monstrous loaf in the middle of the road and then sauntered forward, looking at us with an air of complete aloofness that said, "Smell that shit, bitches!" And damn did it smell bad! We had no choice but to drive over the huge mound of feces. It squished under the wheels and then flew up behind the bus like a big turd explosion. I giggled like a schoolgirl. The manager seemed pissed because he said he was going to have to power wash the entire vehicle before any Guests could get in it. But, whatever. Turds are always funny.

What wasn't funny was that there seemed to be a fucking

turkey leg stand every two feet in the park. By lunchtime I was so grossed out from watching everyone around me tearing into gristle and veins that the thought of eating meat made me want to vomit. I ended up walking around for a good hour looking for decent vegetarian options, and was totally fucking starving when I finally found a place that served really shitty personal cheese pizzas. I ate one of those and some fries and ended up with the worst heartburn of my life. It did not leave me with a favorable impression of Animal Kingdom. I mean, seriously, if you're going to make a whole park about animal conservation and then almost exclusively sell food that contains dead animals, well, that's just kinda fucked up.

We did hit The Magic Kingdom that week, but only briefly. I think we both knew that we were only there to look for Lisa. So it was a bit of a half-hearted visit, although I did enjoy walking backstage at The Haunted Mansion, seeing how all the effects worked.

Nobody at Mouseketeria had seen Lisa in at least two weeks. Someone had heard through the grapevine that she'd punched a Guest, a father who was disciplining his daughter a little too harshly. Another person heard she'd been fired for yelling at a manager. One person said they thought maybe she'd been demoted to a meet-and-greet at EPCOT Center. But nobody had any solid information. The saddest thing was that she obviously didn't have any close, or even casual, friends at The Magic Kingdom, and as a result nobody paid much attention when she'd suddenly disappeared. Like she'd never really existed there at all. A ghost dressed up as Snow White.

Since we were nearby we took the Resort line monorail over to The Grand Floridian to visit with Miss Nancy. We waltzed into the bright majestic lobby, the sound of a piano floating through the air. I didn't blame her for spending all day here. It was so relaxing.

We took the elevator downstairs and spotted a stack of teddy bears' heads peering over the back of a sofa.

"Hey, Miss Nancy!" I said as we walked around the front of the plush couch.

No answer. Something was wrong.

"Miss Nancy?" said Jay.

Still no reaction. She looked pretty normal, except that her eyes were wide open and unblinking, and a white film covered her pupils. She smelled terrible.

"Holy shit," I said. "She's dead, Jay. Way, way, dead."

Jay started freaking out.

"Somebody call an ambulance!" he yelled. He ran to the Front Desk. "We need a doctor over here!"

"Jay!" I yelled. "It's too late for a doctor, you dipshit! She's been dead for days! Maybe weeks!"

He ran back over, stared at her for a full minute, and then collapsed on the couch across from her. I sat down next to him, and then we both stared at Miss Nancy until the ambulance came. They, predictably, pronounced her dead on the scene, and unceremoniously carted her body away.

"She was too old," I said. "Her heart obviously couldn't take the withdrawal."

"I can't believe nobody here noticed she was dead," said Jay, shaking his head.

"She said that if people bothered her they'd get fired. I guess nobody wanted to risk it."

"I saw her a week or so before I was evicted," said Jay. "She came to see if I had any more of The Dust. This was before Theresa tried to sell hers back to me. I told Theresa to sell it to Miss Nancy, but I guess that didn't happen."

"You didn't have any hidden away that you could've given her to help with the withdrawal? I mean, maybe if she'd gradually stepped down the dosage or something…."

"No, I'd been completely out for a week, at least. She offered me a hundred thousand for an eighth. Then she offered me a million. Then ten million. It didn't matter. I didn't have any. Believe me, if I'd had it, I would have just given it to her. I told her if she could front me the money I could get the ingredient, but that it'd take weeks if not months to arrive. I guess she knew she wouldn't last that long.

"She was nice about it, though. She didn't scream or yell or anything. We sat around for a few hours and talked about everyone, and I told her about Lisa, and some stuff about my past that I don't really discuss with anybody. She was a very smart and kind woman who had been through a lot, and she had some really interesting perspectives on my life. It was an... illuminating conversation.

"It's funny.... As I was talking to her I started realizing that I didn't really know anything about her except that her husband had died. But she'd lived quite a life. She pulled out some pictures of herself when she was a nurse at the tail end of World War II, and she was so pretty, Blaine. Just a total knockout. Did you know that she actually knew Walt Disney? Her father ran Red Cross ambulances with him in the first World War. Whenever they were in town, Walt would invite them over for dinner. Her father ended up becoming one of the higher-up execs at Bank of America, and he was instrumental in green-lighting the financing for Disneyland. She told me how she walked through the park before the concrete had been poured on Main Street. And how she knew, even then, that she'd never be able to get enough of that magical alternate reality that Walt had created.

"Anyway, we had this amazing conversation. Then she hugged me and left. And that was the last time I saw her."

"Does she have any kids we can get in touch with?" I asked.

"No. Her husband was impotent. She told me that when she wanted to be around kids she'd just hang out in the parks."

"That's kinda sad."

"It really didn't seem to bother her. She said her husband filled her soul and she was more than happy to devote herself fully to him. That's why she was so crushed when he died."

"Damn," I said.

"Yeah...."

Poor Miss Nancy. That goddamned drug.

"And you're sure there's no more Dust? It's all gone?" I asked.

"Not unless someone else has been stockpiling it. I know there's a guy in Anaheim who makes it, but I imagine he's having the same supply problems I am."

"But you're totally out of it? You swear?"

"I swear. There's none left."

"Good riddance."

A Cast Member walked over to Miss Nancy's sofa, put on latex gloves, opened a trash bag, and started throwing her teddy bears into the bag.

"Hey!" said Jay. "What do you think you're doing with those bears?"

"I've been told to discard them."

Jay looked at me pleadingly. I nodded, and turned to the Cast Member.

"We'll handle it," I said. "We were friends of hers."

"I'm afraid I can't let you do that due to sanitation issues," said the Cast Member.

"Is Phillip the shift manager today?" asked Jay.

"Yes, sir," said the Cast Member, surprised.

"Go tell Phillip that Jay wants the bears."

"It's really not my place to…."

Jay stopped him, his face beet red. I'd never seen him so angry.

"Go tell Phillip I'm taking Miss Nancy's bears."

"Yes, sir," he said, and ran off.

"Little shit," I said.

Jay picked up Miss Nancy's two suitcases, which were sitting next to the sofa. He opened them and started packing away the bears. I joined in and within a few minutes they were all safely stowed away. We each took a suitcase and walked out of The Grand Floridian.

I never went back there again.

Jay didn't seem to give a shit about taking the back route into The Beach Club this time. Still, when we rounded the corner in the lobby and I spotted Charles, I motioned for Jay to go upstairs. But he didn't. He walked up to Charles and gave him a hug. Charles, surprised, hugged him back.

"I don't know if you've heard about Miss Nancy?" Jay asked, breaking away from the hug.

"I did. The Greeter at The Grand Floridian called me a couple of hours ago, when you found her. Damn shame. She was a lovely, complex, wonderful woman."

"She sure was... I wish I'd gotten to know her better," said Jay. "She was like the nice grandmother I never had."

Charles looked down at the suitcases.

"Her teddy bears?" he asked.

"Yes," said Jay. "We knew she wouldn't have wanted them thrown away."

"That was very kind of you, Jay."

"Thanks," said Jay. He paused. "Well, be seeing you, Charles."

"See you soon."

We walked off towards the elevators. I turned back to Charles and saluted him.

Jay passed out on the couch almost immediately after getting back to the room.

I sat in the Jacuzzi for a few hours, drinking wine, and thinking of Miss Nancy and her husband. A strong, successful, smart woman who could have easily gone it on her own, but who loved her husband so much that she enveloped herself in a fantasy world when he died. Could someone have helped her, have guided her out of that abyss? Maybe Charles, if he hadn't been all fucked up himself at the time.

My drunken ruminations turned to Lisa, and about all I'd learned of her grim past. Maybe she was too damaged to be in a normal relationship. Sounded like a life with her would be a constant struggle, always fighting her demons. Was that something I'd be willing to put up with? Living with someone always on the edge of a breakdown?

"Nah, fuck that," I said to myself. "Too many fish in the sea."

I honestly believed it'd be that easy to let her go....

19

—Jay and I maintained our life of decadence for a while longer, sitting on the balcony with Bill the Lizard for days on end, visiting the parks when the fancy struck us, and gorging ourselves at the Concierge Lounge every night, much to Semi-Hot Sandra's dismay. Jay really was an ideal roommate, aside from the snoring. He kept the place clean and didn't complain about anything, which was cool. And it was fun to have a friend around to do stuff with.

But every once in a while he had flashes of extremely odd behavior that would make the hair on the back of my neck stand up.

One time, for example, we were walking the trail between The Beach Club and EPCOT Center, when a cottonmouth snake slithered across the sidewalk. It stopped and hissed at us.

"Step back slowly, Jay," I said. "We'll backtrack and report it to a Cast Member."

But he didn't step back. Instead he snatched it up by its head and turned the snake to face him.

"What the fuck, Jay?! Holy shit, put the goddamned snake down you crazy bastard!"

"I've done this before," he said.

The hand not holding the head choked up on the cottonmouth's body until it was a few inches below the other hand. The snake's tail thrashed, but Jay held it tight. He quickly twisted both hands, and the snake went limp. He threw it into the brush.

I felt sick.

"Jay, goddammit! You fucking asshole! Why'd you have to do that?"

"That snake was a killer, Blaine," he said, completely expressionless.

"Well, now so are you, you son of a bitch," I replied. "It wasn't going to do anything to us! All we had to do was walk away."

"I saved us," he said, with the same flat affect as before.

I got right up into his face.

"Jay, if you ever kill any living being while I'm around, you're gone. You're out of my room. No shit, Jay. I've seen enough death for a lifetime."

And then it was like something switched back on and he was his normal self again, and the snake thing hadn't happened at all.

"Sure, Blaine, whatever you say," he said. He smiled and continued down the path.

Freaky.

A few nights later I was woken by yelling coming from the other room. It sounded like a long stream of curse words. "Fuck you, you fucking cunt whore!" and crazy shit like that. But when I walked into the living room Jay was sleeping soundly.

Creepy.

And then there was the time I noticed him masturbating while watching *The Shawshank Redemption*. Don't really need to say anything else about that one.

Dude was all sorts of fucked up. But I was still too trusting and naïve to worry much about it. I kept bugging him to go to therapy, and he'd always say, "Yeah, sure, I'll go. Make me an appointment." Then I'd make him an appointment and he'd find some excuse not to go. Eventually I stopped trying.

I should have kicked the son of a bitch out of my room. I guess that probably wouldn't have changed anything, though.

His odd behavior was starting to get to me a bit, so I decided to strike out on my own for the day. Figured I'd stroll around EPCOT Center, have a few drinks, and just enjoy the weather.

"I'm heading over to EPCOT Center, Jay!" I yelled from the entryway as I opened the door.

"You want me to come with you?" he asked.

"Nah, I'm cool," I said, quickly shutting the door.

I stepped out of the hotel into what was probably the nicest weather since I'd been there. Crystal clear sky, temperature just warm enough not to need a jacket, and a slight breeze. I could smell the funnel cakes on The BoardWalk over top of the swamp smell. I walked down my usual path to EPCOT Center and thought of the cottonmouth Jay had killed. What kind of person kills a snake with their bare hands? I shook my head, determined not to wallow in negativity today. It was too nice outside, and I was in too good a mood, despite Jay's recent bouts of crazy.

Reaching the end of path, I smelled the funnel cakes again. I wasn't sure I'd ever eaten one, but if they tasted halfway as good as they smelled.... I strolled slowly down The BoardWalk to the funnel cake kiosk and ordered one with powdered sugar, vanilla ice cream, and chocolate syrup. Probably more calories on a single plate than I needed for the entire day. But one good thing about walking around the parks all day, every day, was that I hadn't gained any weight, despite my less than stellar diet of Concierge Lounge food and large amounts of booze.

The first bite of the funnel cake was heavenly. But then the wind coming off the lake started blowing powdered sugar all over the place, so I went and sat down at a table outside of the bakery. I sat there for a while, trying to eat it without making a total fucking mess. It wasn't working. The powdered sugar was everywhere. It was on my face, in my hair, and all over my shirt, a vintage black EPCOT Center number which was now dotted with blotches of white. Fuck. But it was so good. I kept eating.

A familiar-looking couple walked past. I couldn't figure out who it was at first, but then it hit me: she wasn't carrying the towel.

"Michael! Belinda!" I shouted, waving to them. A gust of wind blew the powdered sugar from the now funnel-cake-free plate all over my shirt.

"Motherfucker!" I yelled, as they walked over to me, laughing.

"Quite a mess you're making there, Blaine," said Michael.

"Yeah, man. I'd shake your hand, but mine is covered in powdered sugar."

They sat down at my table as I walked to the nearest trash can and threw away the plate. I walked back, flicking at my shirt, trying to get all of the white blotches off of it.

Sitting down, I smiled at both of them. They looked happy.

"So how have you two been doing?" I asked.

"You have a big piece of powdered sugar right there," said Belinda.

"Where?"

"Here, let me get it," she said, licking a napkin and wiping my face.

"Belinda!" shouted Michael.

"Oh!" said Belinda, pulling back, embarrassed. "Always playing the mother, I guess!" she said.

"It's okay," I said. "So... how have things been?"

Michael pointed to Belinda's stomach. "Somebody is preggers!"

"No shit!" I said. "Congratulations!"

"I'm three months along," she said. She grabbed his hand and they kissed each other.

"That's awesome," I said. "Good for you."

"So, what about you?" she asked.

"Oh, nothing too exciting. Been keeping busy at the parks. Relaxing, enjoying the weather."

"We heard through the grapevine that Jay is staying with you?"

"Yep, yep, that is true. He's been sleeping on my couch for a few weeks now. Just until he gets back on his feet. I'm sure you guys know all about the problems he had with his... uh, supplier."

"Best thing that ever happened to us," said Michael.

"Seriously?"

"It's true, Blaine," said Belinda. "Otherwise I'm not sure I would've been able to get off of it. And I had to get off it! The second I found out about the pregnancy I knew I had to stop. I couldn't be a good mother on that stuff, and I had no idea what it was doing to my baby. Plus, it was killing our marriage. Every time it would wear off, I'd start to feel like Michael hated me. I just assumed he blamed me for our baby dying, and on top of that I felt so guilty for making him deal with all of the... towel stuff. I knew I was being crazy, but it was easier to hold the towel, feel guilty, and take The Dust than go through a normal grieving process.

"Anyway, dealing with all of that, on top of the withdrawal symptoms, was horrendous. If Jay had still been selling it... I think the temptation would have been too much."

"But you kicked it," I said, "and you look great!"

And she did. She was full of color, smiling, and seemed twenty years younger than the last time I'd seen her. And she wasn't being a total crazy bitch. I started to understand what Michael saw in her.

"I couldn't have done it without the love of my life," she said, squeezing his hand. "Knowing he was there for me, and seeing how he loved me so much, and how he took care of me through all of it without complaining.... It brought us a lot closer together."

"Wow," I said. "That's amazing. Really. Congratulations, you two."

I paused, and shuffled in my seat.

"So, um, have either of you heard anything from Lisa?" I asked.

"Funny you should mention her," said Michael. "We were in Epcot yesterday and saw her at the Germany pavilion doing a Snow White meet-and-greet. She didn't look so great, though. I could see some of her tattoos coming through her makeup, and it looked like some of it was rubbing off onto her costume."

I perked up.

"That's great news!" I said. "Well, not about the tattoo thing, but it's awesome that she made it through the detox without losing her job. Sounds like she's not applying the setting powder properly, though. Or at all. Maybe she can't afford it? Anyway, it's good to hear she's still alive. I was really worried about her, and she wouldn't return my calls, and....."

"Sounds like you care for her a lot," said Belinda.

"Yeah, I mean, I guess," I said. "We definitely had some sort of connection. But I haven't heard from her since the morning after the dinner party. Kinda hard to care about a person who obviously doesn't want anything to do with you."

"She didn't look very happy," said Belinda. "Maybe you should go talk to her? She does scheduled meet-and-greets all day."

"I dunno," I said. "I don't want to be all stalker-ish and shit. If she wanted to talk to me she would've called."

"That's not necessarily true," said Belinda. "We spent a lot of time with Lisa over the past few years at Jay's... parties. We grew quite close. There were moments when she would suddenly become very open about her past."

"Yeah, Theresa told me," I said. "Terrible stuff."

Belinda nodded. "She seemed to have a lot of trust and abandonment issues. And coming off The Dust just amplifies whatever problems you were trying to run away from in the first place. I'm sure she was scared to death that if she got together with you she'd just get hurt again. And I bet when you stopped calling, in her mind that probably meant you'd stopped caring, and just reinforced her paranoia about getting involved."

"But that's bullshit. What, was I supposed to call her every hour or something? She would've thought I was a lunatic."

"No, of course not," said Belinda. "There probably wasn't any right way to deal with the situation while she was detoxing. She wasn't going to let you get close no matter what you did. But that doesn't mean you should've given up quite so easily."

"And now," said Michael, "even though she's off The Dust and is hopefully a little more emotionally stable, she probably figures it's been too long, and that you've moved on and don't want anything to do with her. But she's a very sweet girl. I'm sure she feels bad about never getting back to you."

"Yeah..." I said, thinking about what they were saying. "Maybe I will go see her. Maybe I should just act like I'm passing by, and then be all surprised to see her there, and then see how she reacts?"

"Don't do that," said Michael. "The girl already has abandonment issues. Don't make her think even for a second that you forgot about her. Just go up to her and tell her how you feel, and don't leave until she believes it. Don't be a fucking pussy, Blaine!"

"Michael!" shouted Belinda.

"What?!"

"Your future son or daughter can hear every word you're saying!"

"Oops," said Michael. "Sorry."

"No, you're right. I am being a pussy. If I like her, what do I possibly have to lose by going right up and telling her? It's not like she's talking to me now, anyway. It couldn't get any worse. Well, I mean, she could get a restraining order or something, and maybe then I'd get banned from EPCOT Center, and kicked out of my hotel, and thrown in jail for stalking. But other than that, what's the worst that could happen, right?"

"Right!" said Michael.

"Blaine, you're a nice guy," said Belinda. "You have a bit of a foul mouth, but you have a gentle soul."

I blushed.

"Lisa would be a fool to turn you down, especially since she knows you've seen her at her lowest and still want to be with her. That has to count for something, right?"

"Yeah, I guess," I said. I stood up. "Okay. I'll give it a shot. Thanks, you two. Please keep in touch. I want to know the second the baby is born, okay?"

We hugged.

"Bye, Blaine," said Michael.

"Good luck," said Belinda.

I turned and started running towards the International Gateway entrance. Then I stopped running because I started sweating, and I didn't want to be a stinking, sweaty mess when I saw Lisa. Then I started feeling like I was coated in powdered sugar, and my skin got all itchy. Was I breaking out in hives or something? Holy shit, this was an utter disaster. I ducked into the bathroom to the left of the International Gateway, just before the turnstiles.

Phew. No hives. I did have some powdered sugar in my hair, which I picked out. My shirt looked… well, pretty bad, actually. I got a wet paper towel and tried to wipe off some of the stains.

I stared at my face in the mirror for a bit, mentally prepping, trying to get psyched up. I was tempted to do that thing guys always do in movies where they splash water on their face after some really intense moment. I never understood what that was about, though. What good would it do to splash water on my face?

"Ah, why not?" I thought, turning the warm water on. I splashed water all over my face.

Great, now my face was wet. And so was the front of my hair. And also the collar of my shirt. Son of a bitch. Stupid Hollywood.

So, I basically ended up pacing in front of the bathrooms outside of the International Gateway for a half hour while I dried off. But at least it looked like the stains had come out of my shirt.

Resolute, I strode past the bag check, swiped my Annual Pass at the turnstiles, put my finger on the biometric scanner, and entered the park. "I'm a professional. Don't try this at home," I thought, as I walked like James Bond into EPCOT Center, turning right at the top of the hill. I was pumped.

Until I got to the Germany pavilion. Then James Bond ran off like a little bitch and I felt like a quivering bowl of Jello. I needed a boost of liquid courage, so I hit up the stand by The Biergarten and bought a Jagermeister shot. I downed the shot and immediately remembered that I really hated the shit. Great. Now I felt like I was going to spew all over everything. I ordered a Radeberger Pilsner from the booth to wash down the taste of the Jager. And now I was good and soused. Twelve PM in the afternoon and I was drunk.

Whatever. I was ready. I walked straight over to the meet-and-greet area on the far left side of the pavilion, ready to do whatever it took to make Lisa understand how much I liked her.

But she wasn't there. So I stood around for a while, waiting. And then I waited a while longer. My buzz was wearing off. Shit.

I walked back over to the beer stand.

"Do you know when Snow White is coming back?" I asked, feeling like a total pervert.

"One-forty-five is the next scheduled appearance," said the German Cast Member.

"Fuckity fuck," I said. Ninety more minutes. "I'll take another Radeberger, please."

Beer in hand, I walked over to the railing bordering World Showcase Lagoon. I scanned the Germany pavilion and tried to do a mental walk-through of my impending meeting with Lisa. None of the scenarios I conjured up ended successfully. So, the plan was... what? To stand in line behind a bunch of snot-nosed kids, sticking out like a sore thumb, her obviously seeing me way in advance, which would totally mess with her interactions with the kids in front of me? That was awful. And then I'd get to the front of the line and go over to her and have, what, maybe thirty seconds to say something to her? What could I say in thirty seconds? It was a lousy plan.

Or maybe I could wait until she was done and then catch her before she went backstage? Her handler wouldn't be thrilled, but I could deal with him. It'd be pretty weird, though, me just appearing out of nowhere and professing my feelings for her. She'd probably get all freaked out by me surprising her like that and run off.

I turned back to Spaceship Earth. I was in a foul mood and that wand was just making things worse. Why'd everything have to get all fucked up? Things were so much better when I was a kid. Easier, happier, less complicated. I kept staring at the wand, trying to wish it away. Who did I need to pay off to get that damn thing removed?

My pointless ruminations were interrupted by a soft tap on the shoulder.

"Shit, Jay followed me!" was my first thought. Dude was going to fuck everything up.

I turned slowly and saw long black hair.

Jay didn't have long black hair.

"Hi, Blaine," said Lisa.

I gasped, and without even thinking, hugged her as hard as I could. She hugged me back, hesitantly at first, but then tighter. I could feel her body shaking as she started to cry.

I pulled away, wiped her tears, took her hands, and... we just looked at each other. Her eyes had dark circles around them, her skin was breaking out everywhere, and her hair was a tangled mess. She was gorgeous.

I kissed her. And from the way she kissed me back, I knew that all the plans I'd been contemplating, all the speeches I'd been rehearsing... none of them were necessary. Everything was going to be okay. Better than okay. Amazing.

"Blaine, I'm so sorry," she whispered.

"No, no, no," I said, brushing her hair from her eyes. "It was my fault. I should've found you, I should've tried harder to get in touch...."

"I wouldn't have let you," she said. "I would've done things that would've made you hate me."

"Not possible," I said, mustering a smile through my own tears. "Not a fucking chance."

She smiled, too, wrapped her arms around me, and sighed deeply.

Everything I'd been worried and depressed about faded away. None of it was important anymore. Jay and the wand could go fuck themselves.

We stood there for what seemed like hours, just holding each other.

She broke away, finally.

"I have to go, Blaine," she said. "I need to put my costume on and do my makeup. I'm already on thin ice. If I'm late for my meet-and-greet they'll fire me for sure."

"Ah, fuck Disney," I said. "I'm sick of this place. Come back to Maryland with me."

"What?!" she said, taking a step backwards.

"Seriously. We can leave tomorrow."

"I can't just leave, Blaine!"

"Why not? What's keeping you here?"

"My job, for one. I like it here. I get to make people smile."

"You spend all day pretending to be someone else! Hiding behind a character." I pointed to her Dermablend-covered tattoos. "They won't let you be yourself even when you're not on stage! That's not healthy! This fucking place is no different than The Dust. It's an escape from reality. I know it makes you feel all warm and safe inside, but it's an illusion!"

"I know," she said, looking around. "But I think I need that."

"Bullshit," I said. "You kicked The Dust. Leaving this place will be easy."

"But what would I do? How would I live?"

"You could stay with me," I said. I thought of my house, tainted by Sam's death. "I was gonna buy a new place anyway. We can look for one together. We'll find your dream home. Your castle."

Her eyes lit up.

"Really?" she said.

"Really. And you can go back to school, or start your own business, or whatever. I'll support whatever you decide to do."

She hugged me again.

"Is that a 'yes'?" I asked.

"Yes!" she said, and started jumping up and down. "Yes! Yes! Yes!"

I laughed, grabbed her, and kissed her. This was easily the best day of my entire, formerly pointless life.

She pulled away again, and looked at the line forming in front of the meet-and-greet. Little kids stood with autograph books in hand, excitedly awaiting the arrival of Snow White.

"Oh, Blaine...."

"Shit. Fine, I get it. Yeah, go. I've waited this long for you. I can wait a few hours longer."

"Yay!" she said, jumping up and down again. "I'll finish my shift and call you when I'm done. I should be out by ten!"

"Can't wait!" I said. "And that'll give me time to break the news to Jay."

She froze.

"Jay?" she asked, her voice quivering. "What does Jay have to do with this?"

"Oh, yeah, shit. You don't know. His house got foreclosed on, and he's been staying with me for the past few weeks. But he's been weirding me out lately, and the whole situation is giving me a bad Ricky Lu vibe. So I think it was about time for him to move on, anyway."

"Blaine, you don't know him like I do. He has a very dark side. Please don't get him too upset."

"I'm not going to boot the guy onto the street or anything. He's been a good friend to me. I'll pay for him to stay by himself in a single for a while longer, but the dude needs to get his shit together, go to therapy, and get a job."

"He's not selling The Dust anymore?" she asked. Something in the tone of her voice bothered me, but I shrugged it off.

"Nah, his secret ingredient hookup ran dry."

"And he doesn't have any left?"

"He says he doesn't...." I paused, remembering something. "Shit. Now that I think about it, he did tell me that Theresa Skywalker tried to sell her stash back to him a few days ago. I wonder if he took her up on that? I'd be super-pissed if he did. I don't want that shit anywhere near me."

"No, of course not," she said. "Me, neither."

"Anyway, the kids look like they're about to start a fucking riot! Take off, and call me as soon as your shift ends. I can't wait!"

I kissed her, one final lingering kiss, and then she ran towards the backstage entrance, turning to wave before slipping into the darkness. I considered sticking around and watching her do her thing, but I really wanted to get one last final look at EPCOT Center before I left tomorrow.

So, I strolled around the park, trying to soak in all of the sights, sounds, and smells that had meant so much to me as a child. I sat on a bench and watched the sun set over Universe of Energy, as a monorail glided by. It was beautiful, and I'd probably long for it all again, eventually. But now it was time to go. I had what I came here for.

20

—There was so much blood. Jay was covered in it. The walls of the room, the bed, the carpet, they were all stained with blood.

I dialed 911 as Jay sat there, staring at the wall with that insane look in his eyes.

"911. What is your location?"

"The Beach Club Inn, room 5691."

"What is the nature of the emergency?"

"Someone has been murdered."

"Is the suspect still there?"

I looked at Jay. He was pushing his finger against a tattoo on the side of his stomach.

"Yeah, he's here."

"Are you in danger?"

I looked at him again. He was rubbing the tattoo with his finger. What the fuck was he doing?

"I don't know. I don't think so."

"Okay, sir. An ambulance has been dispatched, and the police should arrive shortly. Is it okay if I stay on the line?"

I hung up the phone, realizing it wasn't a tattoo Jay was rubbing. It was a huge gash. The skin had separated, leaving a six-inch oval section of fat and muscle glistening in the light.

"Bitch got me good," he said. "Right over the Little Mermaid tattoo."

The blood wasn't all Lisa's.

I spun around, looking at her seemingly lifeless body, wincing at the sight of her mutilated shoulder, bits of Charles's statue stuck in the gore.

She twitched.

Holy fuck.

A bubble of blood expanded from her nose and burst.

She was still breathing.

I ran over to her. I didn't know what to do. I flipped her over and sat her upright, nearly vomiting again as her left arm almost completely separated from her shoulder. It dangled by a few tendons, her EPCOT Center knuckle tattoos appearing and disappearing as her arm twirled from side to side before finally coming completely off and falling to the carpet with a wet thud.

A red-stained pillow was on the floor next to me. I could suffocate her. Put her out of her misery, like I'd done with Sam.

Fuck that.

I pulled off my shirt and tied it tightly around what was left of the area that used to be her shoulder. I grabbed the pillow and held it against the stump, pressing as hard as I could. I propped her head sideways on my lap. The Haunted Mansion Mouse Ears fell onto the floor.

"Lisa?" I said.

I heard a gurgle in her throat. She was trying to talk.

"Lisa!" I yelled.

One eye opened, and then closed.

Her mouth parted slightly, and blood dripped out.

"Blaine?" she said slowly, in a dreadful bubbling whisper.

"Lisa," I said, crying now. "Don't...."

"So... sorry..." she said. She inhaled, sucking blood into her lungs. She coughed weakly, but not nearly enough to clear the fluid. She was drowning on her own blood, and it was terrifying. "I...."

"It's okay, it's okay!" I said, tears streaming down my face. "Please, just don't die. We're going to live in a castle together, remember? So don't die, okay?"

She didn't respond.

"Fuck that bitch. She lied to you," said Jay, drunkenly, still poking at the gash on his side. "Got off her shift early. Didn't want you to know she was here. Said you two were leaving together, and she needed The Dust to get through the next few weeks."

"That's bullshit," I said, wiping away tears. But I knew it wasn't. I'd stood there that afternoon spouting off my plans for our happy life together, totally ignoring Lisa's concerns about what a huge deal leaving the parks might be for her. She probably should have told me to fuck off. Instead, she came to Jay for The Dust, knowing she couldn't handle such a sudden jump into the real world without it....

What an insensitive asshole I'd been.

Jay tried standing up, wobbled, and fell back onto the bed.

"Bitch fucking ransacked the place," he said, waving his arm across the room and wincing as his wound ripped open even further. "Yelling about how she knew Theresa had given me a bag of The Dust! Ripped the whole damned suite apart, found the bag, and then had the nerve to try to give me her puny life savings for it? Fuck her. I could have gotten millions for it."

"Why didn't you get the fucking millions, then, you asshole?" I yelled. "You could have saved your house! You could have saved Miss Nancy! What the fuck were you holding out for?"

"I wasn't holding out for anything!" he yelled back. "I never intended to sell it! Ever! It was a memento from a big chunk of my life, and I was going to keep it forever, in The Queen's box."

The Queen's box. It had been sitting out in plain view under the TV since the day Jay arrived. I hadn't opened it because I knew he'd freak out. I wondered if the notepad was still in there?

"I didn't end up needing the money, anyway," he continued. "I had everything I wanted right here. A good friend, a nice place to live, people cooking for me... no worries in the world. But this bitch was going to take it all away."

He thrust his finger at Lisa. I nearly jumped up and strangled him.

"You've done a pretty good job of ruining everything all by yourself," I said. "They're going to stick you in prison for years."

I stopped. Prison. He was going back to prison. That fucking bastard.

"You… you did this on purpose, didn't you?" I said, slowly. "You actually want to go back to there, don't you?"

"I'm not living alone, Blaine. I can't do it."

"You crazy son of a bitch," I said. "I can't even begin to fathom how fucked up in the head you are right now."

Jay looked up at me, and then over at Lisa, and it was like he suddenly understood what he'd done. He started sobbing.

"I just wanted it to stay the way it was! I was so happy."

"But this isn't real!" I shouted. "It's a fucking mirage kept alive for the benefit of rich assholes like me! In real life people don't live in fancy hotels and get all their meals from Concierge Lounges and walk around a fucking fantasyland all day! In real life people have jobs, and they make budgets and cook their own food and wash their own fucking sheets!"

"That's not a reality I want to live in," said Jay.

And that was it. There was nothing left to say. So we just sat there until the police and paramedics arrived. I cradled Lisa's head and stroked her hair, while Jay sat with his face in his hands, crying softly.

21

—Lisa was in a coma, and she'd lost a lot of blood. A surgeon performed a clean amputation of her arm in the E.R. There was too much damage to the nerves and muscle, and it wasn't worth risking infection for the slight chance that a reattachment would be successful.

The doctors gave her a 50/50 chance of surviving past the first day. When that day passed and Lisa was still alive, they said they didn't know if she'd ever come out of the coma. And if she did come out, she might have serious cognitive impairments.

But she was strong. I couldn't believe someone could fight so hard through so much pain.

Even though she was still in a coma, after a week the doctors said she was stable enough to be moved out of the Intensive Care Unit. So they transferred her into a nice, sunny, single room. It was on the second floor of the hospital and overlooked a large grassy field. I decorated the room with Disney princess stuff. The staff were all great about me staying there, procuring me a cot and blankets, which was much nicer than the chair I'd been sleeping on in the ICU.

Once she came out of the coma, we'd talk as much as she was able, or I'd read to her, or we'd people-watch out the window, or we'd just sit there, staring at each other. It was like being on a date 24/7. Luckily, everything about her was just as amazing as I'd hoped it would be, and any doubts I'd had about loving her disappeared pretty quickly.

I did cry a lot those first few weeks. I cried when they pulled the tube out of her throat, cried when she came out of the coma, and cried when she turned to me, recognized me, and said my name. The worst was when she finally realized her arm was gone.

"Blaine?" she said, waking me. Her voice was slurring from all the pain meds.

"Hey, Lisa," I said, leaning over the bed. "How're you doing, beautiful?"

"Blaine, I can feel my arm, but I can't move it."

"I know, sweetheart, I know."

"I can't see it, either. Is it under the covers? Can you lift up the blankets for me?"

"Lisa, your arm is gone. They had to amputate it."

"What? Why?" She started crying. "Why would they do that to me?"

"It was Jay, remember? He hit it with that castle statue."

"I don't remember…" she said, drifting off slightly.

"Shit," I said.

I didn't know what to do. Should I be telling her this? Was she going to freak out? Should I get a counselor down here or something?

"Blaine?" she said, slightly more alert.

"Yeah?"

"What about my EPCOT Center tattoos? I'm missing half of EPCOT now."

"It'll be fine, we'll get it sorted out somehow. Don't worry."

"Oh, okay. Thanks, Blaine."

"No problem. Go back to sleep, okay?"

"Okay," she said, and drifted back to sleep.

Yeah, I cried for hours after that.

But from there things got better. It was a slow but steady progression as she was able to stay awake longer, speak more, and eventually move around. Her lost arm seemed to concern everyone else a lot more than it concerned her. They told us that as soon as her stump healed they could fit her with a prosthetic arm. She didn't seem interested until I told her that it'd be a good way to complete her EPCOT Center tattoo set again.

—

Over the course of those three months in the hospital I only left Lisa's side to go to the bathroom and eat.

Except once, when Charles came to visit two days after the incident, carrying a suitcase, a small shoebox with holes cut into it, and The Queen's box. His eyes were bloodshot, like he hadn't slept for days.

"Hey, Charles! Nice to see you! You look like crap, though."

"You're not looking so good yourself, Mr. McKinnon. But it is nice to see you, too."

"No 'Mr. McKinnon', Charles. You're off the clock, remember?"

He smiled slightly, nodded, and went to Lisa's bedside. He watched her breath for a bit, the tube still down her throat at this point. "How's the little lady?"

"Not really sure yet, to be honest. She's had a lot of blood loss and they don't know how that's affected her brain. But, she's alive."

"Such a tragedy. You're lucky you got out unharmed," he said.

"Yeah, I suppose. Sorry about your statue, though."

"Oh, never mind that. It seems so unimportant now."

He turned to the pile of stuff he'd walked in with.

"Well, I brought everything you asked for. Your little lizard friend was right where you said he'd be, sunning himself on that balcony. I'm not sure the hospital staff would approve, though."

I opened the shoebox. It sure looked like Bill the Lizard. I put my finger in there and he bit onto it. Yep, it was him.

"Hey, Bill!" I said. I walked him over to the window, opened it, and set him on the ledge so he could find bugs and get some sun.

Charles slowly handed me The Queen's box.

"Luckily I found this before anyone else did. Are you sure you want it?"

"Not really," I said, taking the box from him and opening the lid. The notepad was still inside.

"Please don't read it, Blaine. I wish to God I hadn't. It's ghastly. I can't sleep. To think I took that stuff…."

I opened the notepad, flipped past the first page, and read the ingredients for The Dust.

It was, as Jay had warned me, truly, truly horrible. Horrible beyond what I'd imagined.

I closed the notepad slowly and looked over at Charles, now completely understanding the pain I saw in his eyes.

"Stay with her for a few minutes?" I asked, standing up.

"Take your time," he said.

I took the notepad, walked down to the hospital's magazine stand, bought a lighter, and went outside. Standing in the street, I held the notepad between two fingers, flicked the lighter underneath it, and set it aflame. When it was burning good and bright I dropped it onto the ground and stood there, waiting until it was all ashes. I went back in, and sat down next to Charles.

"Looks like I'll be making a few calls to some associates in Anaheim," I said to him.

"Anaheim?"

"Jay told me there's someone out there who's been making The Dust."

"Oh, no," said Charles.

"Don't worry," I said. "If I need to I'll spend every last cent I have to track this person down and make sure all traces of the recipe are destroyed. And if that person has given the recipe to someone else, I'll track them down, too. I can make more money pretty easily, but I won't able to sleep soundly until I can be sure The Dust is never, ever, made again."

Charles put his arm around me.

"You're a good man, Blaine McKinnon. A good man. I'm proud to call you my friend."

"Thanks, Charles. That means a lot."

We sat there, looking at Lisa, face bruised and swollen, a stump where her left arm used to be, a tube coming out of her throat. Even through all of that, she was radiantly beautiful.

"I don't think I'm just high on the idea of loving her, like you said I might be. I think I really love her."

He nodded. "I believe you do."

"I hope she's having good dreams," I said.

"I'm sure she is. She looks very peaceful."

We watched her for what seemed like hours, until I drifted off to sleep. When I woke up, he was gone.

We've stayed good friends with Charles. He used to come visit us pretty regularly, but he's been having spine problems, probably from standing all day and carrying peoples' luggage, so he can't travel as often. We still make it a point to go down to Orlando to see him at least once a year, though. And he still sends cards on the holidays. He's doing great. Still working at Disney after twenty-five years (they gave him a Tinker Bell statue for that one), married to Clarabelle, "the cutie" from the gift shop, and... happy.

22

—Belinda and Michael visited a few days after Lisa came out of her coma. Belinda was definitely showing now, which was awesome.

"Hey, I didn't know Jabba the Hutt had a sister!" I said, hugging her, and shaking Michael's hand.

"Blaine!" said Michael, scolding me, but unable to keep himself from laughing.

"You two are terrible!" said Belinda, turning to Lisa. "And how are you doing, dear?"

"Belinda?" she asked, groggily.

"It's me, dear."

"A baby?" asked Lisa, looking at Belinda's stomach.

"A baby," said Belinda.

"Oh, so happy," said Lisa. She dozed off.

Belinda touched Lisa's face.

"Such a sweet girl," she said.

"They keep her knocked out most of the time," I said. "They say her body needs the rest."

"What's her prognosis look like?" asked Michael.

"It changes every day," I said. "I don't think these doctors have any clue, to be honest. Every day they tell me she won't be able to do something, and a few weeks later she does it."

"She's had such a hard life," said Michael. "We're just happy that you're here for her. Most guys would've bolted and never looked back."

"You didn't," I said. "I thought about you two a lot those few first days in here. It was tough, and yeah, there were times when I wanted to run. But I figured, hell, if Michael and Belinda made it through all the shit that life threw at them, maybe Lisa and I have some chance of making it through this."

Michael put his arm around Belinda, and they both smiled at me.

"Enough of this sappy crap!" I said, "Tell me about the damn kid, already!"

"They say it's in perfect health," she said. "I was so worried. I was still on The Dust that first month before I realized I was pregnant, and.... I don't know if I could have handled it if The Dust had harmed the baby somehow. We've already been through so much....."

"I'm really happy for you," I said.

"Thanks," she said, nudging Michael. "Ask him!"

"Ask me what?"

"Blaine," said Michael, "we'd like you to be the baby's Godfather."

"Are you fucking kidding me?!" I said. "Of course! Yeah, I'd be honored!"

"Being a Godfather means you're there throughout the child's life to provide guidance, and to be a moral compass," said Belinda. "Which means you can't curse like that around your Godson!"

"That's fine," I said, "I'd been meaning to work on that anyway. No more profanities! I'll start a curse jar and give the money to the baby! Ten dollars for each curse!"

Five months later I stood next to Belinda and Michael as their baby boy, Adam, was baptized. Afterwards I handed Belinda a check for ten-thousand dollars.

"From my curse jar," I said. "Obviously I've been less than successful. But fuck it. If the kid's gotta learn those words from someone, he might as well learn them from a pro!"

Adam was a beautiful baby, and I was thrilled to be his Godfather.

But there was something very wrong with him.

For one thing, he never cried. He smiled constantly. And while that might sound like every parent's dream child, it was actually kinda creepy. You couldn't tell when he was hungry, or when his diaper was dirty, or anything, because he never cried. He just sat starving in his own shit and piss, grinning like a maniac.

Even stranger was that every once in a while, in the right light, his eyes sparkled like they had pieces of glitter in them. I knew I wasn't imagining this because Lisa noticed it, too. In fact, she felt really uncomfortable around Adam. Wouldn't hold him or anything.

Belinda and Michael put up a good front, but I could tell they knew something was wrong. After a while I started to notice that I never saw Belinda without a glass of booze in her hand.

I hoped to hell Adam was going to be okay. For his sake and for Belinda's.

23

—Nobody had heard from Theresa Skywalker since she'd supposedly run off with Troy Bolton, so I ended up contacting Disney Cruise Line to try to track the two of them down. After a lot of convincing, they gave me the phone number for Troy's supervisor on Disney Wonder. I called and talked to the guy, who confirmed that Troy, aka Sam Katz, was working on the ship in the entertainment division. But he'd never heard of Theresa.

I left my contact info and asked the supervisor to have Troy/Sam get in touch with me. He never did. But a few weeks later I got a postcard in the mail. There was a picture of Castaway Cay on the front, Disney's private island in The Bahamas.

Hi Blaine!

I've been living the life of luxury on a cruise ship with my new husband, Sam Katz, aka Troy Bolton! Wanted to let you know I was okay - sorry I ran off like that without telling anyone. Was so excited to finally find my true love!

Hope you're doing well. Miss you!

Love,
Theresa Katz

"At least she's okay," I said, as I handed it to Lisa.

"That doesn't look like her handwriting," she said. "She used to dot her 'i's with little hearts."

"Weird," I said.

The more I thought about it, the more I realized that something didn't jive. If Theresa was really married to Sam and living on that ship, the supervisor definitely should have known who she was. I called the guy back.

"Hey, I thought you told me you didn't know Theresa?" I said to the supervisor. "I just got a postcard from her saying she's living on the ship and is married to Sam Katz."

"I think I would have known if an employee was married to someone on this ship," said the supervisor.

"Yeah, no shit," I said. "That's why this doesn't make sense. Look, can you go get this Sam dude and let me talk to him?"

The supervisor didn't say anything.

"Hello?" I said. "Seriously, this is freaking me out."

"Sam Katz is no longer aboard this ship," said the supervisor.

"What the fuck does that mean?"

"He didn't return from one of our port excursions in The Bahamas."

"Uh... okay. When did this happen?"

"A few days after we last talked."

"So you told him I was looking for Theresa?"

"I did."

"And you don't think it's a bit odd that he fucking disappeared a few days later?"

"This is an ongoing investigation, sir. I'm afraid I can't discuss it with you any further."

He hung up the phone.

"Goddammit!" I yelled.

I tried for days to get in touch with someone at Disney who could give me information about Sam Katz. Nobody would talk. I even ended up calling the FBI, who said the same thing: "We're not at liberty to discuss ongoing investigations."

Eventually I contacted the Orlando Sentinel. They'd actually published a silly little article about Theresa years ago, sort of like the one they'd written about Jay. The author of the piece remembered Theresa immediately and was extremely interested in what I had to say. He knew some lower-level Cast Members on the ship and ended up getting a few of them to talk anonymously.

Apparently Theresa had been on the ship, but only for a few days. Then she'd just vanished.

"People disappear from cruise ships a lot more often than you'd imagine," said one Cast Member. "Most of them are jumpers. We figured that's what'd happened to her. It was just weird that nobody said anything, and nobody ever came looking for her."

The next day this story was on the front page, and it spread like crazy.

But Disney refused to budge. They wouldn't talk. They wouldn't release their security camera footage from the deck of the ship. Hell, they wouldn't even acknowledge that Theresa was ever a passenger on the ship!

After a few weeks the story died down, and that was the end of it. After that, nobody seemed interested in finding out what had happened to either one of them.

There is a warrant out for Sam Katz's arrest. I hold out hope that he'll turn up someday. Maybe he'll commit some petty crime and get caught, or screw over the wrong person and end up in the hospital with broken knees, or whatever. Because as it stands, he's the only one who knows for sure what happened to Theresa Skywalker.

Did she jump because he broke up with her, and she didn't have any Dust to stave off the loneliness? Or did she get on his nerves so badly that he pushed her overboard?

Maybe it doesn't matter. Because either way, that sad, sweet girl didn't deserve to end up at the bottom of the ocean.

24

—After Lisa was discharged from the hospital we rented a little apartment in Maryland and lived there for a few months while we searched for our dream home. One day I got a bill, forwarded from Charles, for six more months of rent for the storage facility where all of Jay's memorabilia was being stored.

I'd completely forgotten about it.

I consulted with a lawyer, who agreed with Jay's statement that, yes, everything in there was legally mine since it was rented under my name. But I certainly didn't want that crap. I decided to auction it all off, and put the money in a trust fund for Jay's three kids, divided evenly between them.

But before I did any of that, I needed to talk to Jay, one final time. Lisa wanted to come, too, and even though I tried to talk her out of it, she insisted. I guess we both needed some closure.

We walked into the visitation room and were escorted to a booth, where Jay sat behind a pane of glass, handcuffed and in an orange jumpsuit. He looked trim and healthy, and had a new brightness in his eyes and complexion.

"Hey, you two," said Jay, from the other side of the glass. "Didn't think I'd ever see either of you ever again."

"Hi Jay," I said.

Lisa didn't speak.

"Really happy to see you're okay, Lisa," he said.

"Are you blind?" she yelled. "I'm missing a fucking arm you

asshole!"

One of the guards took a step towards us.

"It's okay, she's fine," I said.

The guard stepped back again.

"Anyway," I said to Jay. "I'm not even going to ask how you're doing in here, because I want you to say you're miserable, but I know you're probably loving it."

Jay shrugged.

"There were easier ways to get back to jail, Jay," I said. "You didn't have to hurt your friends."

"I snapped, Blaine. For a few minutes in that room everything made sense, everything seemed very clear. I'm not trying to justify what I did, but at the time, it seemed like the best way out...." He stopped and turned to Lisa. "I know you don't believe me, but I am sorry. I'm not a bad guy. You know that. And I never stopped loving you."

"Jesus," I said.

Lisa just stared at him. Tears ran down her cheeks.

"Look," I said, "the reason we're here is that I need contact information for your ex-wives. I'm auctioning off all of your memorabilia and putting the money in a trust fund for your kids."

Jay looked down, shaking his head, not saying anything for a good minute.

"Hello? Jay!" I said. "Snap out of it. I need that contact info."

"Sure, sure," he said. He motioned to one of the guards on his side of the glass. "Can I get some paper and a crayon?"

He turned back to us. "They won't let me have pencils or pens. They think I'll kill myself. Ridiculous."

The guard brought back the paper and crayon, and Jay spent a few minutes writing down addresses and phone numbers. He gave the paper and crayon back to the guard.

"They'll have to pass that through security," he said. "But just give them your address on the way out and they'll send it to you eventually."

"Okay, great. Thanks," I said. "So just to be clear, you understand that we're selling all of your shit, right? And your kids are getting the money? And you're cool with that? You're not going to try to sue us or something?"

"No," said Jay. "I don't need any of that stuff anymore. I have a new life here. That memorabilia was all from my old life, where everything was stressful and people were always wanting things from me and I had to keep a steady job, and…. Anyway, it's really nice what you're doing, giving the money to my kids. Thanks."

"No problem," I said.

I stood up, getting ready to leave. Lisa stood, too.

"Blaine, wait," said Jay. We sat back down.

"What?" I asked. "I kinda just want to get out of here, Jay."

"The Queen's box?" he asked. "Did you open it again?"

"Yeah, I did," I said. "And that's why I don't feel the least bit sorry that you're in here for life. If you get butt-raped with a fucking shiv every day, that still wouldn't be enough punishment for making that shit."

"Fair enough," he said.

"And just so you know," said Lisa, leaning into the glass, "your partner-in-crime in Anaheim? Blaine took care of him. Nobody will ever be selling The Dust again."

Jay cackled like a goddamned lunatic. It was scary.

"What's funny about that, you son of a bitch?" asked Lisa.

"Oh, it's just that you're both so naïve," he said, smirking. "I've heard of drugs in here that make The Dust look like Pop Rocks. Drugs with a whole list of horrible ingredients, each a million times worse than that one in The Dust you're in such a huff over."

He looked straight at Lisa. "People always need an escape. Isn't that right, Lisa?"

"Fuck you, Jay," she said, and stood up. "I'll meet you in the car, Blaine."

"Still running away, I see," said Jay.

She turned back. Her face was flushed.

"I'm happy now, Jay. I have the life I've always dreamed of. I don't need to run away from anything, least of all your sorry ass."

She shook her head. "You're pathetic."

Jay sat there, stunned.

I stood up, grabbing Lisa's hand.

"Have a good life, Jay," I said. "I wish things could've been different."

Jay was silent, staring into space, oblivious now to our presence.

We left the prison, never went back, and never spoke to Jay again. The auction of his memorabilia netted over two million dollars, which was placed into trust accounts. It was all done anonymously. From what I heard, his family was thrilled to get the money. As far as I was concerned, it wasn't enough payment for a lifetime of dealing with the fact that their father was a sociopath scumbag who loved Disney memorabilia and prison more than his own children. But at least the money would make sure they never had to worry about depending on someone like that ever again.

25

—As cheesy as it sounds, Lisa and I are living happily ever after, just like at the end of a goddamned Disney movie. She found her dream home, an old fieldstone house in a wooded suburb of Baltimore. It actually has a turret on one end. A real castle for my lovely princess. Barf-o-rama, right?

Speaking of barf, I eventually became a full-on vegetarian after the whole turkey leg incident. Literally just stopped being able to stomach the thought of another living creature being killed for my pleasure. Lisa doesn't mind eating the soy stuff, and I figure not eating meat is keeping both of us slimmer and healthier, too. Can't say that I don't totally crave a Geno's cheesesteak every once in a while, though....

Bill the Lizard didn't live much longer. Apparently the average lifespan of that sort of lizard was about one year. He lived at least two, from my calculations.

But one morning, a week or two after we'd left the hospital with him, we went onto the little deck of our apartment and found him sunning himself with four miniature lizard babies. Bill was promptly renamed Alice. I have a photo of the five of them, all hanging from my lower lip at the same time. Chips off the old block, they were, and for years we had her relatives as pets, giving some away to family members as the litters expanded, keeping many for ourselves and caring for them in terrariums when the Maryland weather got too cold. Eventually the bloodline died off, but I always felt good about saving Alice/Bill from that crow, a sort of penance for the lizard I'd stepped on and killed all those years ago.

We got a dog, too, when we moved into the new house. Not a husky, like Sam, but a graying old chocolate lab we rescued from a shelter. We named him Charles. Unlike his namesake, he doesn't do much, just kinda sits around the house, eats, and grunts a lot, but it's nice having a dog again. He does rock a mean bandana around his neck, just like Sam. White, though, not red.

Lisa made a full recovery, aside from the arm, of course. She has an incredibly lifelike prosthesis, which we immediately tattooed with her missing EPCOT Center pavilion symbols. But the prosthesis doesn't do much functionally and is really only for appearances, like if we're going somewhere new where people might be freaked out by her stump. The plastic surgeon offered to make her a hook-type contraption, but she decided against it, saying it'd be more trouble than it was worth. She did a bunch of physical therapy for a while, and that seemed to go a long way towards making her fully self-sufficient.

Most of her time lately has been spent going to school for a BA in psychology. She eventually wants to become a substance abuse counselor, which I'm sure she'll be great at. She also volunteers as a Big Sister for kids in a local foster home. They adore her.

I couldn't be prouder. I love her more than I've ever loved anything, and it's the best feeling in the world.

We're still not married, though, and neither of us is too anxious to have kids. We've never explicitly talked about it, but I think she's scared our baby would turn out like Adam. I guess I am, too. We could always adopt, though.

Anyway, it doesn't matter, because right now we're just happy spending every day enjoying each other's company and being "grown-ups" for the first time in either of our lives. Cooking together, going on trips, watching movies, walking around the neighborhood, and having lots and lots of what I personally think is pretty mind-blowing sex.

I do buy Lisa a teddy bear every year, on the anniversary of the day we first met. We have a nice display case with all of Miss Nancy's bears neatly arranged in it, and we're gradually adding to the collection. I'm looking forward to watching it grow....

It's not all sunshine, of course. She has her bad days like everyone else. Hers just tend to be a lot darker than most people's. We'll see something on TV that reminds her of Xanadu, and next thing I know she's in the bedroom, curtains closed, sobbing in the dark. Sometimes she stays there for days. She goes to therapy every week, but refuses to take any meds, which is understandable, I guess. Hopefully as the years go by there will be fewer and fewer of those dark days. But she can't forget her past, and I don't expect her to. For better or worse, it made her into the person I fell in love with.

I've taken a bit of a different path in life than I expected: I'm a bestselling self-help author and motivational speaker, which I find utterly hilarious considering I literally can't go more than two minutes without dropping an f-bomb. Anyway, on a lark I wrote a book called *Life After The Pursuit of Money,* which basically talks about how making money should be a means to an end, not the end in and of itself. It's pretty silly stuff, actually, but I get flown all over the country to speak in front of executives from Fortune 500 companies about work/life balance, how a number on a paper isn't worth anything if you're not happy, and how building up a bank account without using the money for anything positive is the same as hoarding stacks of newspapers ... or Disney memorabilia.

People seem to like the way I talk, fucks and shits and all. Those corporate guys get a real kick out of it. The owner of the largest social media site in the world, a billionaire a few times over, recently told me I should go into politics. Maybe I will. Maybe I'll even run for President some day. I mean, a President who tells Congress to go fuck themselves on live TV before vetoing their bill? Yeah, I'd probably vote for that guy.

But I'll tell you the best thing to come out of writing the book: revenge. Sweet, sweet revenge. See, Ricky Lu had been MIA since my breakdown. Couldn't find any trace of him. Even hired a detective. No luck. Then one day I was doing a book signing, and fucking Ricky Lu appeared out of nowhere and out asked me for a job. Seriously.

I didn't skip a beat. I took down his contact info, shook his hand, and told him I'd be in touch.

A week later he was busted for possession of child porn, which he swore wasn't his. What a strange coincidence!

EPILOGUE

—In August, shortly after we'd moved to Maryland, I got a call from Charles.

"Blaine, come back to Walt Disney World. You need to see this."

"Is everything okay?" I asked.

"Sure, everything is spectacular. You are going to love this."

So, Lisa and I hopped on a plane the next day, returning to Walt Disney World for the first time since that horrible night.

I felt weird about going back. It had been the paradise of my youth, but now every time I thought of the place, all I could picture was Lisa's bloody stump, Jay's crazy tattoos, and that goddamned wand. Paradise lost, indeed.

Charles met us at the Transportation and Ticket Center at The Magic Kingdom, along with Clarabelle. Michael and Belinda were also there with baby Adam.

"This way, everybody," said Charles as he led us all up the ramp to the EPCOT Center-bound monorail. He talked to the pilot, and motioned us to the forward-most cab. We had front-row seats.

The fifteen minute ride was pleasant enough. We all just sat there in silence, Charles beaming. I wasn't looking forward to the final loop around Spaceship Earth, though…. The glittering crimson stars at the end of the wand reminded me of The Dust sparkling against Lisa's blood.

"Charles, I don't want to see this shit again. It's depressing."

"Just you wait, Blaine. Just you wait!"

We rounded the final corner and the park came into view, Spaceship Earth filling the curved window of the monorail.

I gasped.

There was a crane attached to the side of the geosphere. We passed by the crane just as it ripped a huge section of the tip of the wand from its base and swung the red star-studded twist of metal safely past the globe, before dropping it unceremoniously to the ground with a crash.

"They're tearing down the wand!" I yelled. "There is hope for the future!"

Lisa snuggled up to me, and as I turned my head from the glorious destruction above, I saw her face framed by an amber and blue Florida sunset, and the beauty of the moment was nearly overwhelming.

I looked around at my smiling friends, and my strong, luminous Lisa, and felt that only then, at long last, was I truly a rich man.

But I wasn't living in some naïve fantasyland anymore. I knew there would still be hurdles to overcome, and struggles against the pain meted out by the random cruelty of fate and the inevitability of death. Except now I understood that the wisdom and serenity gained from pushing past such obstacles, not alone, but with the help of loved ones like those surrounding me... well, that was the stuff of a full life well-lived.

I couldn't wait for what lay ahead.

ACKNOWLEDGEMENTS

Our Kingdom of Dust either wouldn't exist or would have sucked major ass without the help of the following people:

—Hugh Allison, my editor and fact checker, for sending me pages upon pages of extraordinarily helpful notes. Hugh has an encyclopedic knowledge of everything WDW, and a keen eye for spotting the hallmarks of lazy writing, be it plot holes, voice inconsistencies, grammar and spelling mistakes, or run-on sentences, such as the one you're currently reading. I wouldn't have felt comfortable releasing this book to the world of Disney fandom without his help. Find Hugh at www.hughallison.com.

—Brett Bennett, Jeff Heimbuch, Newmeyer, Ron Schneider, and George Taylor, for pre-reading the book and telling me it wasn't the terrible embarrassment they'd expected. Thanks also to Eva Maler for giving it a proofreading from a non-DisNerd point of view.

—Davida Gypsy Breier, W. Patrick Tandy, and Gregg Wilhelm for graciously and generously sharing their deep knowledge of the publishing industry with an annoying newbie.

—Jonas Kyle-Sidell, for once again doing a bang-up job on the layout for the paperback. It looks like a real book!

—Alan Partlow, for driving down from NYC to shoot the cover, and for not complaining when we got fake snow all over his gear. Check out more of his work at www.alanpartlowphotography.com

—Draven Star, not only for her amazing work as the cover model, but also for being a hilariously fun travel companion, drinking buddy, and dear friend. Looking forward to getting into trouble at WDW with her for years to come. Keep up with her DisNerdVentures at www.doomdoll.com

—Pentakis Dodecahedron, for designing a perfect cover, helping to prop up my self-esteem whenever I felt like my writing was complete shit, and generally being the kindest, most loving life-partner a guy could ever hope for.

—My mother, for inadvertently funding the research for this book years ago by purchasing Three (and Four) Season Salute Passes for me and my sister. I didn't realize how lucky I was at the time, but EPCOT Center was pretty much the coolest fucking playground ever created, and she knew it.

—All the fans, websites, blogs, and podcasts who helped make *The Dark Side of Disney* such a huge success. Your support and appreciation motivated me to get off my ass and write a follow-up. I know this isn't what you expected, but hopefully you'll like it anyway!

—And, of course, Uncle Walt and all of his Imagineers, for creating paradise.

15189401R00111

Made in the USA
Lexington, KY
17 May 2012